BLEAK

J. PARKER

BRONZE BELL
PUBLISHING

BRONZE BELL

PUBLISHING

Bleak by J. Parker

ISBN: 9788396468918 Paperback
ISBN: 9788396468901 eBook

Text by J. Parker
www.jparkerauthor.com
Cover art by Damonza

THE PHONE CALL

It wasn't too late in the evening, but the dinner guests were already pretty drunk. It was a celebration of Hannah's return to health, and because she couldn't drink herself yet, her friends made sure to drink her share.

The scar left by the surgeon's scalpel itched under her silk dress. After a while Hannah found it more amusing than annoying. It was an itch proving she was still alive. And she wasn't supposed to be.

Heart surgery is no easy matter, and she counted herself lucky that she was the mayor's wife. She had that vague idea that if not for his connections, the surgery wouldn't have been arranged in time to save her life.

Her saviors sat next to her—her husband Mark (considerably drunk) and Doctor Montgomery, The Man Who Mended Her Heart. As libations progressed, Mark's face was becoming redder and redder, while Doctor Montgomery drank moderately and spoke rarely.

Probably not a social person, Hannah thought. *Especially not in such a colorful, noisy crowd.*

Her husband had insisted on inviting as many people as possible to her party—artists, sportsmen, politicians, "people who mattered." And she insisted on inviting only her closest friends, explaining she was too tired to entertain a party of more than ten. Thankfully, she won.

This small gathering was still very, shall we say, energetic. The assembly of fashion designers, painters and TV personalities was loud, obnoxious, and—in Hannah's naïve assessment—charming.

"To the bravest woman in the world! To her recovery and her long, healthy life!" said Luis, an actor, embracing Hannah and raising his glass of cognac.

"Hear! Hear!" Glasses clanged around the table.

She nodded, raising her own glass, filled with cranberry juice. Alcohol did not mix well with the medicine she was prescribed after her surgery. She humbly accepted all the toasts and boisterous good wishes accompanied by alcohol fumes. The one party where she needed to be sober was all Hannah needed to realize how irritating her friends were when they were intoxicated.

From time to time she jealously eyed Doctor Montgomery whom Deidre, with cheeks reddened by liquor, tried to engage in conversation. He was so calm and polite while she yelled at him about the latest fashion trends. The doctor's indifference to Deidre's mortifying behavior impressed Hannah. At that moment she truly envied the talent to be unfazed by someone's lack of manners.

"Phone call for you, ma'am," her housemaid said to her ear, distracting Hannah from her thoughts. "Mr. Sally."

"Who?" Hannah frowned. She was sure she didn't know any Mr. Sally.

"He wishes to congratulate you, ma'am on your recovery."

The phone was several rooms away from the dining room where the party took place. Each passed room and closed door deepened the silence that Hannah embraced with a sigh of relief. She was more tired than she was ready to admit. Mr. Sally, whoever he was, was doing her a favor.

She picked up the receiver and chirped in a fresh, cheery voice: "Hello? Mrs. Jacobi speaking."

"Good evening, Mrs. Jacobi." A grating voice scraped her eardrums so unexpectedly, she flinched. She'd never known anyone with such a voice—so tired, and so…

Sad?

No.

So resigned.

"My congratulations on your full recovery."

"Thank you," Mrs. Jacobi replied mechanically. "I'm sorry, Mr. Sally, but your name has escaped my memory. Could you please remind me how we know each other?"

"You have a lot in common with my wife, Mrs. Jacobi," answered the voice without even the slightest change in tone.

"Oh? So I know your wife," said Hannah politely.

"No. I'm just saying you have much in common with her."

Silence fell like a heavy theatre curtain when the rope snaps. Hannah was completely dumbfounded, unable to find a fitting reply. She said nothing and neither did Mr. Sally for a while. All of a sudden she realized the grandfather clock standing in the room was ticking very loudly.

"Good night, Mrs. Jacobi," Mr. Sally rasped with a fake politeness, and the phone call ended.

"What on earth was that?" Hannah frowned.

The grandfather clock struck nine—time for her pill. She fingered for her pendant, a delicate piece of pearl and gold she wore on a chain around her neck, and popped it open. A bunch of little white pills rattled inside. The doctor said she should always chase one with a glass of water, but she decided to ignore his advice this time. The pill was tiny, easy to swallow without a drink.

The phone call upset her, but the silence around her calmed her easily. She had never enjoyed being alone, but the surgery made her appreciate it more. Those short periods she spent by herself, marveling at the very fact of existing. Just a bit longer, and she'd go back to the party.

The phone rang again.

"Hello? Mrs. Jacobi speaking."

"What medicine do you take?" The grating voice of Mr. Sally made her shiver.

"The medicine I need after my heart surgery," surprised by the question, she answered without thinking.

"Is that what they told you?" Mr. Sally scoffed. "Pray tell, Mrs. Jacobi, if you had heart surgery, why were you cut open all the way down to your stomach?"

Hannah's heart leapt to her throat. Instead of thoughts, white emptiness filled her skull. How could he know that?!

The phone call ended once again.

Her blood running cold, limbs jerking in nervous spasms, mind empty and stunned, Mrs. Jacobi marched upstairs to her and her husband's bedroom. Her movements quick and tense, she shut the door and sat on the bed.

Next to the bed stood a mirror, big enough for Hannah to admire herself from head to toe. Looking straight into it, she breathed heavily, while the room around her spun.

She unbuttoned her dress and let it slip down, leaving the upper part of her body naked, bar a thin brassiere.

From between her breasts emerged what had been a surgical cut, but was now a nasty scar. An itchy, ugly line of spliced flesh running between her ribs, over her belly and ending just above her womb.

She'd thought about it before and couldn't understand. She knew nothing about surgery so why would she question Doctor Montgomery. And yet, if she had heart surgery, why was she cut like that? And what did Mr. Sally know?

"…For she's a jolly good fellow, for she's a jolly good fellow! Where is she?! Where's Hannah?!" Her friends were singing when she came back to the dining room. A roar of applause welcomed her when they realized she'd joined them again.

It took an hour, a long agonizing hour, before her friends and her husband let her be and she could talk freely to Doctor Montgomery. She invited him to come with her to the next room to converse in peace—followed by Mark's suspicious gaze.

"Doctor. I need to ask you an important question. I decided not to before, because I didn't mean to question your skills as a surgeon, but there is a detail that keeps bothering me."

"Which is?" The doctor's voice was like the sound of a tuba, always claiming all the attention to itself.

"Why was I cut all the way down to my stomach?"

After the question came the silence. She tried to read Doctor Montgomery's face, but it showed nothing: not a twitch of a muscle, not a twinkle in the eye. Unmoving. Indifferent.

But thankfully the mouth started talking.

"I am very sorry, Mrs. Jacobi. It was a terrible mistake on the part of my hospital's staff."

"What mistake? If there was a mistake during the surgery I should've known about it right away!"

"The mistake was the way you were cut." Doctor Montgomery reached for an amber box hidden in his pocket. He took a pinch of snuff and applied it to both of his nostrils. "The surgeon who prepared you for my surgery made the wrong incision."

Hannah's head spun.

"What do you mean 'surgeon who prepared me?' Don't you make the initial incisions yourself?"

"Not as per hospital policy, Mrs. Jacobi."

"We didn't want to tell you," her husband's voice interrupted them. Mayor Jacobi stood in the doorway, completely red in the face, but surprisingly lucid.

"Joel told me about the mistake right after your surgery and said he would accept any consequences, moral or financial. But how could there be any consequences?!" Mark gently closed his hands around Hannah's white fingers. His gaze, drunk but filled with love and affection, melted her heart just as it did so many times before.

"How could I persecute a friend who saved the life of the creature that is dearest to me? I decided not to tell you. I was certain you would ask about it sooner or later, but I preferred later, just so you could regain your strength to have this argument. And I'm glad that we're having it! I'm ready to have a thousand more because you're alive to have them with me!" He lifted her hand up to his lips and left a kiss on it. How lucky she was to have such a loving husband! And Mark was right—what's a stupid wrong incision if she's alive and well?

"You're right," she said, gently freeing her hands from her husband's grasp. "I'm sorry—"

"Oh, don't be sorry!" Mark chortled nervously. "You have every right to be upset! But I'd like to ask you to forgive Joel for this slipup. After all, he performed a miracle."

Hannah turned her gaze toward Doctor Montgomery and smiled warmly.

"I forgive."

A knock on the door prevented the doctor from replying.

"Mr. Sally on the phone again," said the housemaid. "He asked if you would like to continue your conversation, ma'am."

"Who's Mr. Sally?" Mark looked at Hannah inquisitively.

"Oh, don't you remember, dear?" Hannah turned on her cheery voice and instantly felt guilty for being so shameless and deceitful. "Before the surgery I was looking for a new gardener and Mr. Sally was one of the candidates. He called to congratulate me on my recovery and somehow we began talking about the best soil for roses."

"Perhaps I don't remember—" Mark turned suddenly grouchy.

"Oh, please, darling! I'm so bored when I can't drink! Let me have that conversation."

Without waiting for an answer, she trotted several rooms away to the phone.

"They keep lying to me!" When she picked up the receiver again, she was close to tears. "I can tell! Are you willing to tell me the truth?"

"Let me tell you about my wife, Mrs. Jacobi." The hoarse, tired voice scratched on her eardrums. "And a little bit about myself."

"Florentine worked difficult jobs. Scullery maid, they would call her. Then cleaner at the Hospital of God's Mercy, where the good Doctor Montgomery reigns supreme, was the first stable job in her life.

"The money was finally good, but Florentine would overwork herself. We wanted to have a baby, and she said she needed to earn as much money as possible. So she worked for many hours a day, sometimes eating very little or nothing. I could not take care of her, you see, I was working at the docks, and my shortest shifts were twelve hours."

My God, Hannah thought. *There are people living like this!* she closed her eyes to stop the tears.

"But she was much weaker than me. One day she lost consciousness while on the job. When she woke up, she lay on a hospital bed and Doctor Montgomery was sitting next to her, measuring her pulse and listening to her heart. He even did some blood tests, all for free! He said that Florentine was healthy, but she needed to eat more frequently. She adored him after that—you can imagine.

"Then one day Florentine came to me. 'I have a proposition,' she said. 'It's a difficult one.'

"When she told me about the 'proposition' I called her crazy and forbade her from returning to the hospital ever again! There was… a patient to be operated on. Some important person, we figured. They never said their name.

"Montgomery asked my wife because she had the same blood

type as the patient. And the request was… for a kidney. The money he offered would be enough for us to buy a house and have not one, but three children. But I thought that no man of morals would ask for a piece of someone's body for a price."

"She went anyway," whispered Hannah.

"Right you are, Mrs. Jacobi. She went and she never came back. So I searched for her. At the hospital they told me they hadn't seen her for several days. When I tried to talk to Doctor Montgomery and mentioned my name, he turned away and practically ran. I apologize for my lie, Mrs. Jacobi, but I could not risk giving you my real name at first. Peter Buckberry, pleased to meet you.

"Since Doctor Montgomery didn't want to talk to me, I yelled after him about the proposition he gave my wife. That made everyone around me turn against me. I was told that 'such outrageous accusations' toward Doctor Montgomery or anyone else from the hospital staff would not be tolerated. I was kicked out.

"Then I went to the police. I didn't tell them about the kidney thing, afraid they would kick me out as well, but I told them about my wife going missing and that she worked at the hospital. They were very reassuring and helpful, and after taking my testimony they sent me home, advising me to take some rest and promising they would do what they could to help.

"The very next evening I went to the police again. I spoke to the same policeman. This time, he was scared. And not of me. He said he couldn't help me and that my wife probably escaped with a lover. I was shocked. Just a day before he'd reassured me he would do everything to find Florentine.

"When I insisted on him helping me, he threatened that I could either get out or be jailed for an assault on an officer of the law. Then I understood. I might work at the docks, but I'm not an idiot. I left the police station. On my way home I pondered who might have enough money and power to not only arrange a disappearance, but also to keep the police silent.

"An even more painful and terrifying surprise awaited me back home." Up to this point Mr. Buckberry spoke fast, as if to ensure Hannah heard it all. Now the same voice shuddered and broke. She could hear how he fought against his tightened throat, forcing the words out.

"On the kitchen table… under a white hospital sheet… lay Florentine… naked, cold… pale… So beautiful even in death… Next to her—a bag filled with money and a death certificate stating that Mrs. Florentine Buckberry died of heart failure. And that was it. The message was clear—this is what we're paying you for, take the money and shut up."

Mr. Buckberry whimpered. Hannah parted her lips, trying to find the words. But no words were the right ones…

"I checked the body. There was a surgical incision beginning between Florentine's breasts and ending above her womb. I'm no doctor, but I was sure it was too big of a cut to take just a kidney. Just like your cut is way too big for heart surgery, Mrs. Jacobi.

"The next day the newspapers screamed: 'Mayor's wife miraculously recovering from a difficult heart surgery! Doctor Joel Montgomery's biggest triumph yet!' I connected the dots. And sneaked into the Hospital of God's Mercy while Doctor Montgomery was out. Nobody paid attention to a simple man wandering around hospital corridors. Even those who'd seen me before apparently already forgot my face."

"Honey, is this Mr. Sally still?" Mark entered the room, clearly vexed.

"I can hear your husband, Mrs. Jacobi," said Mr. Buckberry.

"Finish this!" Hannah pleaded to the receiver, her blood leaving her cheeks and limbs. She shot a terrified glance at her husband. She needed the truth!

"The documents I found in Montgomery's office listed details about an unnamed female patient marked as 'of the utmost importance.' A patient with the same blood type as my wife. A patient suffering from multiple organ failure. Everything inside that woman went to shit, pardon my expression, Mrs. Jacobi. The only chance of survival—multiple organ transplant. Chance of surgery success: five percent. And the last note in the documents: 'donor found.'"

"Darling, what is going on?" Mark's voice turned from annoyed to threatening. He made a few steps towards her, but stopped as Hannah raised her finger warningly and snapped, "Not. Another. Step!"

Her husband froze in place, clearly as surprised by her behavior as she was.

The voice from the receiver turned into a trembling mumble. But Hannah understood the words all too well, no matter the difficulty with which they were said.

"I came back home and I… cut her open… Took the scissors and… Every stitch… I… She was empty inside!" A burst of hysterical laughter straight into her ear made Hannah flinch. "Everything was taken! Lungs! Heart! Kidneys! Stomach! Nothing was left!"

The phone fell to the floor as Mark attacked, trying to knock the receiver out of her hand. There would be no way for Hannah to win a wrestling match against her husband if he was sober. But that time they struggled for a bit and finally locked in an embrace, both equally exhausted.

"Good evening, Mr. Mayor," the voice from the receiver turned falsely polite and cold. "I suspect it is you who has joined the conversation."

"You piece of shit! How dare you harass my wife?!" Mr. Jacobi roared in fury, his muscles still working against Hannah's.

"I thank you for the generous reimbursement for Florentine's life. You are a much better provider than myself. It's amusing how money and connections make all the difference in the world. And luck, I guess. Mrs. Jacobi still only had a five percent chance of a full recovery. I guess Doctor Montgomery really can perform miracles."

"You'll pay for this, you son of a bitch!" shouted Mark.

"I wish you a long and healthy life, Mrs. Jacobi," said Mr. Buckberry in the gentle voice of a person resigned to their fate. "Please remember that you and my wife have much in common."

Before either Mr. or Mrs. Jacobi found their next words, the sound of a gunshot from the receiver pierced the air. The thud of a dead body falling to the floor followed. And the silence fell.

Mayor Mark Jacobi picked up the phone, placed it back on the table, and looked at his wife. He was solemn, looking for the right words, if such existed for this situation. Hannah looked back, tears rolling down her cheeks. She clenched one fist on her stomach, the other on her chest, filled with terror and disgust at the knowledge of what was inside her.

Before any words could be spoken between the two, a joyous yell from across the house broke the silence:

"For she's a jolly good fellow! For she's a jolly good fellow! For she's a jolly good fellooooow! And so say all of us!"

HOUSE ALIVE

ALICE HAD BEEN awake for quite a while. How long? She couldn't tell. Half an hour? An hour? There was nothing in the house that could tell her about the passage of time. All the clocks were still. No birds in the garden. Not even a cricket. Nothing alive except for the plants in the greenhouse. And the house itself.

After long consideration, she plucked up the courage to open her left eye just a crack to check on the amount of light entering her bedroom through the window. Yep! It was morning alright! A grey, cloudy, disgusting morning. She took a look at the dust hanging in the air. Not floating. Hanging. Everything in this horrid mansion was dead and still.

She quickly closed her eyes again, startled by a noise downstairs. A rumbling sound like a controlled earthquake. Shit! The house had noticed she was awake.

Just leave me the fuck alone! she thought, pressing her eyelids tightly together.

The rumbling again. This time like a ferocious animal running through the corridors, banging from wall to wall, ramming everything on its way. It sounded like the complete devastation of the ground floor. And yet, when she went downstairs, the house would be in perfect order.

Today she was feeling rebellious. Today she wasn't going to listen to the house.

"No!" she yelled to the emptiness filling the rooms. "I don't want to get up yet!"

Another noise. Incoming footsteps so loud she was sure the sound itself would crack her skull. And the door to her bedroom, previously slightly ajar, began slamming repeatedly: WHAM! WHAM! WHAM! as if a child was throwing a temper tantrum.

Alice covered her head with a pillow, pressing it firmly against her ears.

WHAM-WHAM-WHAM! A steady torturous rhythm drilled into her skull.

"STOP IT!" she yelled from under the pillow, and the slamming ceased as abruptly as it began.

A tear dropped from her eye and sank into the sheet.

"I'm... I'm up!"

She had to work against her muscles to get up, as they'd shut down in protest. Her mind was completely blank as she approached the old enamel bowl sitting on a dresser. The water inside the bowl was so old you could count the particles of dust trapped on its surface. Days ago she would have shuddered at the thought of using that water to "clean" herself. Now her mind was numb. She splashed some of it on her face and wiped it with an old t-shirt she left on the dresser.

Downstairs, in an old dining room, breakfast was waiting for her. The coffee was black as ink and bitter—her supplies of cream and sugar ended weeks ago. Not only that, the coffee was far from freshly brewed, but cold and tasted like it had been made from stale beans. Luckily, Alice had her dry toast to numb her tongue against the nasty taste.

Eons ago she had eggs, ham, and cheese for breakfast. But she already ate all that—she hadn't counted on being held captive for weeks. All that was left was stale coffee beans and bread. Maybe she'll get to die of starvation?

She couldn't focus on happy thoughts for too long, because the meal was quickly over, and the house did not like her to sit still and do nothing.

"Going to work now!" she announced to the emptiness, leaving the breakfast table.

❧

It had seemed like such a good idea! An old mansion in the middle of nowhere, abandoned, unguarded. She looked it up one day on the internet and was bewitched by its Victorian gloominess. She loved every branch of withered climbing rose, every chipped brick. She loved the shroud of fog embracing the house in the evening, and the inner greenhouse where plants grew unspoiled by human hand. What a perfect place to find inspiration for her new series of paintings! There was only one problem…

She couldn't afford to rent it. She didn't even know if the house was available for rent. She never contacted the owners, if there were any owners, and she never told anybody where she was going. She packed some clothes and food, her easel, and all of her painting supplies. She crammed that inside her tiny wreck of a car and arrived at the mansion.

Two weeks! Alice thought. *Two weeks and I'll have a masterpiece! And enough sketches to last me for twenty more!*

After a month of imprisonment she ceased counting days.

Her easel was set up in the greenhouse, where she wanted to paint her "Ghost Amidst the Roses." What was meant to be a semi-transparent figure amongst splashes of blood red, was now a mess of colors and shapes, as she doodled on it for days on end. Her passion for painting had died when she realized she was a prisoner, only a week into her presence in the house.

For the first week she didn't leave the mansion. She could open most of the windows (some of them were so huge, she wouldn't dare try, though). Sometimes she took a walk around the building to look for inspiration—she was disappointed there were no graves around the house. Then, one day, she wanted to open the window in the dining room—the one she was opening each and every day of her stay. It wouldn't budge. She blamed it on humidity, even though the house was as dry as an old bone lying in the summer sun. And she encountered the same issue with every single window she tried: the ones in her bedroom, the ones in the kitchen, the ones in the library.

A bit worried, Alice tried to open the front door, which she had used for the past several days. It wouldn't move either. She pulled and pushed, she fumbled with the doorknob, she banged on it, all in vain. She had a moment of panic, then she remembered that she originally entered the house through the greenhouse door.

With her heart racing she rushed to the greenhouse, and when she tried turning the doorknob, her heart sank. It was like the knob was decorative, fixed in place. Once again, Alice attempted to force her way out—she lifted a heavy flowerpot with a dead aloe vera inside and threw it at the glass wall. The heavy flowerpot shattered, but the glass…

The glass was intact.

Bewildered, Alice approached the greenhouse wall. She wiped the earth smeared all over it and fingered its surface. Not a crack. How?!

She tried another flowerpot, then a hammer she snatched from a workbench. Again—nothing. The glass was immune to any and every force she tried on it. With a hoarse shout of anger and frustration, she went back inside the house, took a heavy bronze statue (a replica of Michelangelo's David) and rammed it into the greenhouse wall. The head of the sculpture popped off, leaving the poor David closer to the Winged Victory of Samothrace, but the glass remained indifferent to the assault.

There was a throbbing pain in Alice's chest. She sank to her knees, her fingers freeing the statue, which fell to the floor with a metallic thump. Her mind went numb, and she curled on the floor, weeping.

The sound of a bell filled the air. A happy, jingly bell. Unnerved, she followed the sound to the dining room. There was breakfast waiting for her on the table. Coffee with cream and sugar, ham and cheese sandwiches, and an apple cut into small wedges, the way she prepared them each and every morning. The only trouble was—she hadn't prepared them this time.

"Hello?" she asked the silence. Nothing, no one. Only a small brass bell with a handle, sitting next to a plate. She sat down, eyeing the meal like it was a venomous snake coiled on the table. Was it possible that she had prepared it herself and forgot about it?

Clearly she was taking too long to begin her breakfast, because the house shook a little. A growling sound grew around her as if the room was a stomach rumbling from hunger.

Alice clutched the table, startled, and wouldn't let go until the tremors ended. Earthquakes didn't happen in this region, so she couldn't comprehend what had happened. A local sinkhole? Some nearby mine, perhaps?

A single bell jingle made her jump up in the chair. The brass bell. It hadn't moved, and yet it made a sound.

"I'm making things up in my mind. It must be the isolation," Alice said with a weird relief. "May as well eat something."

As she sank her teeth in the sandwich, a pleasant, cheery sound filled the air. The sound of porcelain and crystal chandelier clinking with joy, probably as a reward for doing what she was expected to.

Seeing the swinging chandelier and shaking porcelain, Alice muttered, finally realizing: "The house is alive!"

~

She put another splash of red paint on the canvas. Another splash that in no way helped the composition, another splash that just ruined the painting that was supposed to be her masterpiece. She didn't care. When she was pretending to paint, she could let her mind go numb. She could make another angry move with a brush, dreaming about setting the house on fire or leveling it to the ground with a bulldozer.

That particular day she was preoccupied with the thought of dying from starvation. The house was clearly running out of food, and it didn't seem like it could make more. Thinking about dying filled her with mixed emotions. Satisfaction that she would finally be set free from the house, yet angry because she was way too young to die.

Furious thoughts raced through her brain. She blamed herself for the idea of living in the house illegally; she blamed herself for not talking to anyone about it; she blamed herself for being a useless, stupid bitch!

She threw the brush onto the floor. It rolled, leaving a trace of red. Silence fell, so complete and so ominous, Alice could hear her blood circulating in her veins. She stood up so abruptly, the stool she had been sitting on fell over.

"I need a break!" she snapped at the corridor that rumbled at her. Conflicting emotions made her eyes water. Not wanting to cry, she pressed her eyelids together, resulting in painful pinching. Sniffing, Alice wandered aimlessly through the building.

She ended up in a library. The flames were roaring in the fireplace, and the smell of old books almost made her gag, but there was little to gag with.

She sat in a rickety old chair and fixed her gaze on the fire. What was the extent of the house's powers anyway? It could move its insides, no matter if that was to ignite the fireplace or make her breakfast. Did it have any power in the garden outside? Was the iron gate the limit of its kingdom?

She browsed the documents left on the desk. Most of them were herbology and gardening books, but one was a notebook filled with handwriting. She engaged in reading it, hoping to learn something about the house. Maybe something that would tell her what was going on.

It was the diary of a gardener, detailing the cultivation process and growth of different saplings. She flipped the pages with scribbled notes and sketches of various plants, followed by recipes for teas, infusions, syrups, and even salads. Most of them for uninteresting purposes—weight loss, fertility, better sleep. One for an upset stomach, another for a headache, the next for a sore throat. And then there was this:

I cannot take it anymore. The house will not let me go free. It keeps me here, so it will not stand by itself in this wasteland. It was a mistake to stay here after Ed's death. I never thought a house could be more lonesome than a human.

A sole rumble shook the far side of the corridor. A warning—it was nearing dinner time. Alice ignored the noise and continued reading.

There is no way out, no escape other than death. It will feed me with whatever's left, and give me water, so that I'll live this pointless existence like a moving piece of furniture! I hate it! I hate it! I HATE IT WITH ALL MY HEART!

Another rumble, this time in the middle of the corridor.

Yesterday I attempted to set fire to it, but it was no use. It controls any fire inside it. I wonder if it could extinguish flames that were set up to its exterior, but I have no way of checking that.

Several pages were torn out and the next available sheet of paper began with:

I decided to end it. One way or another it will end when the brewing process is finished. I used all of my herbology knowledge and created a new recipe. The effects include: unconsciousness, paralysis of the body, slowed heart rate and breathing. In other words—a state that simulates death. I hope the house has no love for dead people. I hope I'll be thrown away like a broken doll and then I'll be free. One has to be extremely cautious with the proportions, otherwise death may not be simulated.

The rumbling approached the library door and shook the floor so powerfully, the carpet bulged out in a wave that glided from the entrance up to the chair she was sitting in.

"I'm coming, I'm coming!" she hissed impatiently, putting the notebook away.

At the dinner table all that awaited her was a glass of water and a single slice of bread on a fancy dinner plate. She looked at it and smirked.

"Is that all that's left?!" she asked the dust hanging still in the air. "I'm now eating the last of the food?!" Somehow that amused her so much, she laughed. The sounds coming from her vocal cords were not her usual high-pitched laughter, but more of a dog's bark. She lacked air in her lungs, her mouth was dry, her body ached, and she collapsed on her knees, cackling like an insane person. She curled into a ball, sank her fingers in her black hair and pulled it out in clumps, howling hysterically, because her end was coming.

And the house won't have any power over me anymore.

That evening the rumbling she heard while lying in bed was her own empty stomach. She lay on her back, eyes fixed on the ceiling above. She felt relief, because her suffering would be over soon. She felt sadness, because she wasn't quite ready to go. She felt sadistic satisfaction, because the house would lose her. And she felt fear, because she expected that dying of starvation was a long and painful process. The sleep that followed was a prelude to death—losing consciousness to never wake up. She hoped her end would be more or less like that.

Morning welcomed her with steel-gray skies. Despite fireplaces lit all around the house, she was cold. She had already lost weight, for weeks fed with leftovers, but she also had no clothes for colder months.

She splashed some water onto her face and forced herself to go downstairs to the dining room. She found exactly what she expected: a glass of water and an empty plate. Yesterday evening she thought about chuckling at the sight of it, just to spite the house. Now, with a pit in her stomach, craving something to munch on, she had no reason to laugh. She drank the water and went to the library.

In there she went back to the diary. The previous house owner described the process of creating the "fake death" potion in detail. Not that Alice would need that—death was coming for her anyway. Till then, she needed to pass the time, so she searched for more notebooks with the same handwriting. She found one at the bottom of a pile littering the floor. There she read:

For the behavior of the house I have no explanation. It is difficult for me to even use that phrase: 'house's behavior.' None of my closest or extended family was ever spiritual or religious and I find no reason for the obvious sentient nature of the building. I can only say with an utmost degree of certainty that the house wasn't always like this. I studied the old almanacs and diaries of my family and I have found no proof, not even an anecdote, that could point to the house ever behaving this way. Or behaving at all.

It is a fact that many past members of my dynasty have died in this house. Since I have to acknowledge the existence of the paranormal, I decided to conduct a spiritual séance. I would like to emphasize here that I do not condone this sort of entertainment. In the current situation, I reckon, it raised to the rank of scientific experiment. The purpose was to determine if the building is occupied by any spirits, ghosts, or other entities that could prevent me from leaving. If I performed the séance correctly—and considering my natural meticulousness I am sure I did—there is nothing sentient in the house, not a human soul, nothing that could be called a demon, angel or other. The house is silent, yet still alive.

Some hours later, dinner bell interrupted her lecture.

This is a joke! she thought, her stomach churning.

She walked toward the dining room thinking that at least she could drink water. Or maybe she shouldn't? Death from thirst would be quicker and she doubted it would be more painful than the hunger pains she had already.

In the entrance to the dining room she froze. There was a pitcher of water, just as she expected, but there was also something on the silver diner plate: a tiny splash of yellow, not like any fruit or vegetable she knew.

Coming closer, she recognized it was a bird—a goldfinch. She knew that one, because she painted birds quite a lot when she was younger. It lay on the plate unmoving, wings sprawled, and its legs up. It was still fully feathered, with its beak and eyes and everything else in place. It was just dead. On a plate between a fork and a knife. A tiny puddle of blood formed around its neck, wrung so violently, the veins broke.

"What am I supposed to do with this?!" Alice whispered in terror.

A slight rumble made the plate jingle, and the dead bird shook like a cat's toy.

"I! AM NOT! EATING IT!" she yelled so loudly the words scraped her throat. "I'LL DIE FIRST!"

This time the rumble shook the entire chamber, and Alice ran. She wanted to reach the stairs and hide in her room (as if it was any safer). But the quaking floorboards made her loose her footing. She fell to the floor as ceilings and walls trembled around her, doors slammed, chandeliers swayed above her head.

"NO! YOU HEAR ME?! I SAID NOOOOOO!"

When she sat again at the dinner table, her body was bruised all over from the picture frames, antlers, and other decorations that fell on her. Her lower lip was cut and had just now stopped bleeding, and Alice was certain her elbow was sprained from the impact. Not the impact of her fall. The impact from the blow she'd received when an invisible force lifted and threw her at the corridor wall. Shakingly, she reached for the bird carcass sprawled on the plate. It still had crumbs of soil and pieces of foliage stuck to its feathers.

She took a single feather at the tip of the left wing between her pointer finger and her thumb and picked it. Raw. The goldfinch was raw. And still warm.

"I'd... appreciate... if you could cook them next time," Alice stammered with effort. "Can I ask you for that?"

A subtle jingle of expensive porcelain in the glass cabinet assured her that it would be so.

Alice plucked the feathers, one by one, from one side of the bird, and sank her teeth into it, ripping it open, with a crunch of tiny bones breaking under the weight of her jaw.

The blessing of meat in her mouth suddenly overcame the disgust, the sorrow, and the pain of her own flesh. Her brain was telling her that she was doing good, and that she enjoyed it. What a traitor! All in all, your brain is not your ally when it comes to higher purposes.

She picked the meat from between the feathers, and reached with her fingers for the insides, warm and slimy and not as gross as she expected. Her brain was drowning in serotonin, her stomach growling with joy, as it again had something to digest. Beautiful! So she'll live another day!

Sometime later she lay in bed, defeated both in flesh and soul. The house had won yet again.

And Alice was too tired to shed a tear.

Next morning three mice, burnt to a crisp, awaited her on a silver plate. She nibbled on them for a whole hour, too famished to feel disgust. After breakfast (after which she hoped she would die from some contagious disease carried by the rodents) she took the notebook of the previous owner from the library and headed to the greenhouse.

She strolled along old flowerboxes and flowerpots, looking for the plants sketched on the pages containing the recipe. Everything necessary for the creation of the fake death potion was still there. In the corner of the greenhouse she also found an ancient chemistry set, the same that the notebook's author used—dusty, but in perfect condition.

The same day she began the process of pretending to be the new devoted caretaker of the house. She believed it necessary so the house wouldn't suspect anything. After all, the last owner vanished after producing the potion. The following desperate entry was the last in the notebook:

> *The brew is finished. I'm putting these last words to leave the proof of my doing. In a matter of minutes, I'll be dead or free. In either case it will be close to impossible to write another note after the deed is done, for if I succeed, I have no intention of ever returning to this accursed place. I will never cross the threshold of this hellish mansion ever again, not even in an attempt to destroy it. My soul is broken, and the moment I get free, I will disappear forever. If anyone ever becomes a prisoner like myself, and finds this notebook: wish me luck and I wish you some in return.*

Alice walked around the greenhouse, doing what she suspected gardeners usually did—cutting down some excessive growth, watering the soil, and mumbling to herself about how the poor plants had been left all to themselves for so many years. She also did some work in the library, putting the tomes piled in heaps around the desk in their right places on the shelves, hoping to find more handwritten notebooks. Wandering around the mansion, she dusted this and that and began cleaning the chemistry set left in the greenhouse.

In the following days, between eating and regurgitating roasted crows, boiled rats, and baked sparrows, she tended to the plants, favoring those useful for her purpose, and step by step prepared what was needed for the brew. She dried some plants, boiled others, measured the proportions, and consulted the notebook. Alice was no cook or chemistry specialist and following the instructions was extremely difficult for her. She experienced no satisfaction, no hope, and no fear. Her mind was constantly numb, her heart indifferent. She only knew she was doing the one thing still under her control.

In a week the greenhouse was engulfed in the bitter smell of the brew. If Alice could feel anything, she would probably fear the house would recognize her actions as the same as the last owner, and punish her. But the house did nothing. Perhaps she overestimated its intelligence? Or maybe the mansion was all too happy with her caring for its insides to worry?

And then the day came.

Alice sat in the greenhouse, fixing her empty gaze on a cold, colorless sunset. The grass outside was crunchy with frost. Not that she could experience it by herself, but that's how she imagined it—crunchy.

She sat next to the chemistry table and listened to the perks of the brew. The bitter smell, similar to a herbal tea but ten times stronger, made her nose ache.

An old-fashioned clockwork timer was in working condition, and she set it to fifteen minutes according to the instructions. When the timer rang, her movements were stiff and robotic. She took the little pot from the burner and poured the liquid into a ceramic mug. The mug was white with a cartoon kitten playing with a ball of yarn. *Cuteness overload*, it stated. She considered it extremely tacky and impractical, but she liked it because her mom gave it to her. She was also sure it could contain the exact amount of the brew she needed.

She poured the liquid through a strainer to catch all the leaves and petals floating in the mixture. And she let it cool. Not because she cared about burning the roof of her mouth, but because *cool to room temperature* was the last instruction. And there it was: death in a mug.

After some minutes she hovered her hand above the surface of the potion—it seemed lukewarm. She picked it up, sat up on her knee, and gazed at the light-yellow, semi-transparent liquid. Such an inconspicuous thing! It looked and smelled like a herbal tea, and probably tasted not much different, considering its ingredients.

She tried to convince herself she was about to drink chamomile tea, not that she ever did that. She hated tea.

What if she'd made a mistake? What if she mixed up the proportions or used the wrong plant? And even if she did everything right, she had no idea if this would work.

Her body didn't shake, but her arms, cradling the mug with the poison, locked in place. Her brain didn't know much, but it did know what she was holding.

So many thoughts galloped through her brain. *Maybe there is another way?! Maybe I'll grow to like it here? Maybe I should buy the house's trust and it will let me go outside someday and then I can escape? Maybe the owners will come back sometime?*

She looked once more at the last rays of sunlight reaching her from above the gray pines and lifted the mug to her lips.

The liquid was colder than she anticipated. And pretty much void of taste, which was surprising, but made it easier for her to drink the entire mug in one go. And that was it! She set the mug back on her knee. She waited, her heart racing in horror from what she had just done. Alice counted seconds.

One, two, three… absolutely nothing.

Ten, eleven… *my heart's racing, but that's just stress…*

Sixty… nothing… but there was no description of how quickly the potion would work…

One hundred and twenty… perhaps she screwed it up?

Three hundred… apparently she did.

She sighed heavily, relief and pain flooding her soul simultaneously. She would need to plan something else. But first, she needed to go to bed. The house would be angry otherwise.

She stood and her stomach suddenly twisted like a startled snake. She yelped in pain and dropped the mug on the floor—it broke with the crisp sound of fake porcelain. Her stomach jerked and growled, stirring up the brew inside it. THE PAIN!

A wave of pain flooded her insides. Hundreds of daggers

pierced her abdomen, then twisted together, then hooked onto different parts of the tissue and pulled!

She hollered in agony, collapsing on her knees. Stomach juices erupted and Alice coughed. The stain she left on the floor was red! Alice wiped her lips and with terror beheld her fingers slick and shiny with blood. For the love of all the gods! She was dying!

She thrashed her fingers deep into her throat to induce vomiting. And she did vomit more blood. The brew was by now assimilated into her veins and running through her body.

"NO!" she yelled inside her head, unable to make a sound among all the retching she did. She choked on her own blood and on her own tears. She crawled on all fours but was losing the feeling in her limbs. Paralysis was coming!

Like a toy running out of battery power, she ceased moving. She fell nose down on the ground, still conscious. Rapid movements of the stomach stopped, taking away the pain. Alice's breathing slowed, which evoked another panic attack. She couldn't make herself breathe faster, though she really tried. Her heart was slowing as well. She became very cold.

And then she flew. Her body became weightless, her senses merged with air, freezing cold came over her and numbed her skin. Her eyes wide open, she saw different shades of darkness, then the ceiling was passing above her quickly, lit by the candlelight. Sometimes a stern face from a portrait sized her up with disappointment. She entered emptiness and lost all of her senses: hearing, sight, smell, and touch. She was still conscious, and that was the worst. The inside of her head was the only reality she had left. Heart beating like a raindrop falling from a leaf, breaths as a grain of sand tumbling from a dune, she passed out, or at least she thought she did. She died.

❧

Something was burning her back. The sensation came before the realization of what it meant. Alice had her senses back. Her breathing and heartbeat were again steady and normal. She had a taste of salt and iron in her mouth and her stomach hurt like an open wound. And she could move her fingers! Better! She could move her entire body!

She sat up slowly, muscles burning. A wave of sizzling pain ran down her back—frostbite. She'd been lying on the ground all night. And now the unwelcoming, steel-gray sky was again lit with fall sun.

Feeling like a mummy coming back to life after thousands of years of slumber, she turned her head toward the house. Tears escaped her eyelids, pinching her skin. She lay on the ground outside the outer wall, right under the iron gates, cast away like a broken doll.

With difficulty and little cooperation from her aching body, Alice stood up. She sized up the building from top to bottom, and heard a rumbling coming from inside. An angry, desperate rumbling. The house saw her, and realized its mistake. The front door opened like a pair of arms longing to embrace someone...

Alice backed up in panic.

Her car stood next to the front porch, hidden in the bushes, but she wouldn't risk trying to get it. She turned her back on the house and started walking. Her stomach hurt as if a firecracker had exploded inside it. Alice treaded with difficulty, but still carried herself away from the hell she'd endured.

Behind her back, the house opened all its windows and let the wind howl a longing, beseeching note. She only quickened her pace. The porcelain and the chandeliers jingled a tune of temptation—she let go of her stomach and covered her ears. She stopped crying from fright when the house disappeared behind a curve of the road and the pines muffled its screams.

~

In the evening she reached the nearest town—the last one she'd passed through on her way to the house. It took a while before an ambulance came from the next town over and carried her to the hospital. Her mother arrived in the morning, then her sister called from her flight back to the States.

Alice told the police there was little she could remember. She remembered being held captive, force-fed, and finally poisoned and abandoned. She never saw the face of the person who abducted her; that person also never spoke to her. The residents of the little town pointed out the direction she came from, and her car and belongings were all recovered. There was the canvas with blobs of color left here and there (Alice stated that the abductor allowed her to paint, but obviously she wasn't exactly into it), and her blood staining the floor. The culprit was never found, and in the end the case was dropped due to lack of evidence.

The house stands to this day.

SUPERSTITION

The winter was especially harsh that year. By November fields were covered in a knee-deep snow. In the middle of December the first horse-pulled sleigh crossed the river, so thick was the ice. After New Year, farmers from more remote households were isolated from the town completely. Residents of the town maintained tunnels in the snow to allow passage between houses, the market, and church, but those living farther away were unlikely to be seen again before the spring thawing.

The Guiscard family was one of those isolated. They had an even bigger surprise when a human shape emerged from the forest in the north. They wouldn't have noticed if not for the dogs barking incessantly at the stranger floundering through snowdrifts. Cyrille and Grandfather carried him inside.

The man was almost frozen to death. Only the thick sable fur in which he was clad saved his life.

They sat him next to the fire and covered him in blankets. It took an hour before the survivor's hands ceased to shake and became stable enough to hold a spoon.

The man's name was Berger and he was of nobility, one could recognize that by the way the monsieur was clothed and adorned with jewelry on top of the way he spoke. Berger wore three rings on his right hand, and two on his left. Each almost cost him a finger, embracing his flesh with freezing cold precious metal, but Berger didn't take them off, not for a second. When given goulash, he ate slowly, even though he was famished.

The spoon traveled without haste between the bowl and Berger's mouth, feeding him meat and gravy. He deplored having to hold the dish in his hand. There was a table in the room, but the peasants hadn't thought about asking him to sit at it, or pushing it in his direction, so he could eat like a human being while enjoying the warmth of the fire. But what could be expected from those who had not grown far from the animals they breed.

There were six of them. Mee was three years old, and Berger suspected that on a usual day she was noisy and annoying as all peasant's children are. Only now, scared of a stranger, the little girl was observing Berger from under the table, gnawing on a piece of clean cloth. Jean was eight years old, and was a healthy, average lad, slowly saying farewell to his childhood and being engaged in more and more household chores, building up his usefulness to the farm.

Sophie was fourteen, and at first Berger pondered why a girl this plump and pretty was still at her parents' home instead of being married. He understood when he saw Sophie standing up from her bench—she had to use a walking cane (or, to be more specific, a carved stick) to move around. Her skirts reached the floor, but Berger was almost certain one of her legs was shorter than the other. Despite that, Sophie moved a lot, and moved fast. She could easily keep up with everybody else, including her younger siblings. There was something about her that made Berger both curious and suspicious. That air of reverence that often accompanied village midwives and other hags knowledgeable in the ways of herbs and forest demons. Berger decided to keep a close eye on her.

The oldest of the children was Cyrille, nearing seventeen years of age, doing his best to fill the shoes of the man of the house. The husband and father of the bunch was gone. Berger suspected he had been drafted into the army and sent to fight in Portugal, or possibly Spain, and never came back.

The mother of the four, and the widowed wife, was plain and insignificant in her appearance and deeds. Berger never learned her first name, as she presented herself only as Mrs. Guiscard. Finally there was the grandfather, Marceau Guiscard, lanky and dry. He resembled a twig that could be snapped over the knee, and his lower lip shook when he wasn't talking. Despite of that, he still moved about the house with the energy of a teenage boy, though his strength was obviously not like the old days.

After eating and warming up, Berger explained to the Guiscards that he had been traveling to Javols. On the fifth day of the journey the coachman lost his way in the snowstorm. The first of the two horses pulling his carriage broke its leg while descending a hill—they left it for the wolves. The second horse dropped from exhaustion a day later. It took Berger two days to reach Guiscards' farm. His coachman and servant succumbed to the elements on the way.

The grandfather listened, shaking his jaw in contemplation. Cyrille was frowning, trying his best to appear decisive and confident, and when Berger finished, it was he who spoke:

"Monsieur will stay with us until the snow thaws and the road is clear enough. We have a sleigh and a horse. The nearest town is half a day away, and Javols—another day. Till then, Monsieur can sleep in the room upstairs. Sophie! Prepare the room for our guest!"

At first Sophie seemed to ignore her brother, not acknowledging his order in any way. But after a while she marched to the upper floor and for some time they could hear her bustling upstairs. Meanwhile Cyrille and Marceau talked to Berger about the possibilities of recovering his luggage. During the conversation, Cyrille left to head upstairs. At first Berger was convinced that he did that to help his sister, but then he heard both Sophie and Cyrille speak in raised voices. He understood only one angry yell of Sophie's:

"No! It's Father's!"

After the argument Berger heard Sophie bustling again, but this time, right above his head. When she came downstairs again, long after Cyrille did, her face was contorted in an expression of anger and disgust.

When Berger was guided to the upper floor, a bed with a thick quilt and plump pillow was all ready for him—it was right above the fireplace and the chimney went through that room, so it was the warmest, the most luxurious room in the house. *Good! These people know their place.*

Exhausted and with chills in his back, Berger lay down to sleep. The pillow and quilt were far less comfortable than those he was used to—rough to the touch and smelling of straw. Regretfully, none of that could be helped. He decided to just fall asleep and pray for the snow to thaw at least a little.

Something woke him in the middle of the night. At first he was sure he heard a wolf howling outside and that made him cringe beneath his covers. Quickly he realized it wasn't a wolf, but a dog yawning. The air was so cold and clear, and the silence around so perfect, Berger could hear it all the way from the barn as if the mutt lay down beside him. And then silence overcame the farm once more.

Very few people understand how complete silence can be. Berger did not understand—he spent most of his life in cities and was used to constant noise, no matter the time of day or night. But now…

Now there was nothing and it was so unreal. He needed a second to understand where he was and how he got there. He took a good long sniff—the smells of straw, feathers, rough fabric, and wood filled his nostrils. He listened for the sounds of the house, but it was unnaturally quiet. Not even a sigh a sleeping person sometimes makes. If not for the moonlight entering through the window behind his back, illuminating part of the floor and the closed door to his room, Berger would believe he was suspended in a void.

And then a sound, finally! From downstairs. The creak of a wooden floorboard. A very normal thing: a footstep. But who was walking around the house at this hour?

He pondered where the footsteps started and concluded it was by the fireplace. Slow, deliberate footsteps came up to the flight of stairs, stopped, then began ascending.

So they're taking turns watching the fire, Berger thought. *And the time has come to change shifts.* He tried to guess who was walking out there. The footsteps were way too heavy for Mee or Jean. It couldn't be Sophie, as there was no walking cane thumping rhythmically. That left only: Cyrille, Marceau, and Mrs. Guiscard.

But they sounded like the footsteps of an adult man, healthy and strong.

Somehow Berger became uneasy, so he tried to distract himself with being annoyed. *These peasants can walk as much as they want during the night, because nothing less than a slap to the face can wake them, but I'm a much lighter sleeper!*

He was terrified, and couldn't say why. There were many superstitions to explain why people suddenly felt fear, one more blasphemous than the other. But it was a fact—his blood froze, his skin covered itself in itching goosebumps. He cringed, hoping to hide under the quilt. The steps came up to his door!

Silence again. As perfect as before. Maybe he was dreaming? That must've been it. But all of a sudden, all the racing thoughts, all the explanations ceased. For the door slowly creaked open…

An ear-piercing squeak of rusty hinges. Berger hoped it would wake somebody, for his own voice got stuck in his throat. He begged his body for any kind of sound to come out of his mouth, but there was nothing. The moon shone on the emptiness of the corridor.

Berger's eyes hurt from salty tears. There was nobody! The silver rays of moonlight now reached the door on the opposite side of the corridor, but there was nobody between his door and the next one.

He blinked and squinted and tried to figure out if he was maybe lucid dreaming…

And the door slammed shut!

With a weak yelp Berger shot upright in his bed. It was morning, and the household was filled with noise again. The door to his room was closed, and his pillow was damp from sweat. His breath turned into steam—the whole house was cold.

Strange that the stairs didn't creak when he was descending them. Come to think of it, the door to his room didn't squeak either. But because of that, his appearance was a surprise to those already gathered downstairs in the one and only room that constituted the ground floor. And only because it was a surprise, Berger could see what the Guiscards surely didn't want him to see.

He saw Sophie taking a bowl from the stool he sat on yesterday, right next to the fireplace. The bowl was filled to the brim with goulash and she poured it all into a huge old pot hanging in the fireplace. A fireplace, only now being lit again by Cyrille.

Berger decided not to let them know he saw, so he went back up a few steps and descended again, this time thumping loudly.

"God bless you!" He nodded in the direction of the two startled children.

"And bless you, too," Cyrille and Sophie replied in a mechanical, trained manner.

During breakfast Berger behaved innocently, as if he saw nothing. He chatted and ate, and thanked the Guiscards for their kindness. And inside his head he told himself there was no God in that house. That goulash was left for someone who could no longer eat.

After the morning meal Cyrille guided Berger from one farm building to another to present their humble household. Berger pretended to care for the cows and pigs, but in his mind he was arguing with all the Guiscards at once. He'd heard about the superstitions cultivated by some of the peasants of the southern provinces. Ghosts of beloved ones who died too early were believed to still inhabit their houses and help their families. Such a ghost had to be fed and given a place to rest. What Sophie had said the night before: "It's Father's!" had a new meaning—Berger had been given a room left to the deceased.

A furious expression contorted Berger's face. *Disgusting nonsense in the land of God! Some inferior minds will never learn!*

He thought about forgiving them, as they were little more than the cattle they were keeping. By the time he was wandering the farm on his own, as Cyrille had to get back to his chores, his mind was set to leave them be. Poor beasts!

Cyrille had shown him the direction to the nearest town, and Berger took a walk to the border of the farm to stare longingly at the horizon. He was in a rush to reach his uncle's house, especially since he'd sent him a letter to announce himself in advance. His uncle would be worried.

Possibly the news already had reached his uncle—false news about what Berger supposedly did back in Toulouse. Uncle was the only one who could save him and his position. And now Berger was stuck in the middle of nowhere. Perhaps they'd announce him dead? He didn't want to be dead! He wanted to be very much alive and with all of his privileges. But he needed his uncle to pull some strings.

And now this! God knows how long I'll have to stay with the Guiscards! And what's going to happen to my titles and possessions, while I'm stuck here, without any possibility of defending myself!

His eyes stung as salty tears gathered on his lower eyelids. But his sorrow was interrupted by a pair of voices:

"...We almost froze to death, that's what it is!" Cyrille's voice was loud, angry, and unrestrained. Berger was hidden from his and Sophie's sight by a thicket.

"You shouldn't have angered Father!" Sophie reprimanded her brother. She didn't scream, but spoke in a way mothers scold their children. "I told you that I would be happy to give away my and Mee's room, but you had to give a stranger the best, the warmest place in the house! So now you have it! Father did not eat, and did not keep up the fire! Now don't blame me!"

"What was I supposed to do?!" Cyrille hissed in frustration. "You saw the way he is dressed! If I did not give him the best room, he would notice, and—"

"And give you less money for his rescue?" finished Sophie with an ironic smirk.

"Mother is right! You **are** impertinent! That's why you're not married yet!"

"I'm not married yet because I don't want to be! And Father will be displeased as long as this stranger stays in his room."

"I cannot ask him to move now! You must talk to Father!"

"And why should I? It's your fault he's angry at us!"

"Because Father will listen to you!"

"It's you who deserves to hear a thing or two about respecting your parents!" Sophie chuckled unpleasantly.

"And because if you don't talk to Father, I'll tell Mother you volunteer for nightly fire keeping for the rest of the winter."

"She won't believe you."

"She won't, but she'll have no other choice than to appoint someone if Father is unwilling to keep the fire up. Mee and Jean are too young, Grandfather is too old, and myself and Mother do most of the chores—"

"No, you do not, you lazy donkey!"

"We'll see whose side Mother will take!" Cyrille was now skipping away, laughing. Sophie followed him, calling him names.

Finally, Berger was alone again. And he was sure he could not just let these people go unpunished.

From the moment he lay down to sleep that night, Berger prayed like he never had before. At that point he was certain that what he experienced the night before was a feverish dream sent upon him by the witch of the house, Sophie. She was angry her older brother hadn't indulged her wish of leaving the room to her dead father. There was no way a human soul could be wandering around earth before Judgment Day—such preposterous beliefs were simply sinful. But he learned it wasn't only Sophie's belief, but the entire family's, so he was even more disgusted, and his mind was made.

First, he needed to survive another night. So he prayed, sweat dripping from his forehead. The entire house was asleep already, and he was praying, fixing his gaze on the moonlit doors.

Finally, in the dead of the night, he heard footsteps. These were Sophie's for sure, because of a distinct thump of a walking cane. They stopped at the top of the stairs, and then, from the ground floor, another set of footsteps came up the stairs and stopped right before her. Berger cringed under his quilt—what kind of a demon had that witch conjured up?

"Good evening, Father," Sophie spoke softly, but in the silence embracing the house her voice was like a scream. "I'm so, so sorry we offended you."

She paused. Berger listened carefully, but the answer to Sophie's statement was only silence.

"I know, but Cyrille means well. It's hard for him to act as the man of the house."

Another moment of silence.

"That's what I told him! But he rarely came to you for advice before, and he still hesitates to do that now."

Silence again.

"I hope so, too! Cyrille wanted me to convince you to keep the fire up at night, but… can we do that together? I really need to talk to someone sensible."

This time the silence was broken by the sound of footsteps, both Sophie's and someone else's.

Hugo Berger, the heir to the Berger fortune and name, and the Bishop of Toulouse, prayed intensely for the salvation of his soul until sleep did not soothe his aching mind.

❧

A knocking on the door woke him. Before he even retrieved his full consciousness, Cyrille was already in his room:

"The snow has thawed enough for us to travel to town!"

Not half an hour later Hugo Berger, in a sleigh pulled by a single horse, with Cyrille at the reins, left the farm, and each and every member of the Guiscard family sighed in relief. The very next moment all the bedclothes Berger had used were washed thoroughly and hung next to the fireplace to hopefully dry till the evening.

Mee and Jean, forced to keep quiet for the past day, could run and laugh freely again, and the adults dropped the masks they wore for their guest. Mother smiled again, Grandfather whistled while feeding the cattle, and Sophie decided to not give Cyrille too hard of a time after his return.

They waited till the sun set and lit the torches in front of the house to make sure Cyrille would find his way home. And when he came back it was Jean who took care of the horse, and Sophie who brought her older brother his meal. They all went to sleep after a big chunk of roasted chicken, slaughtered just for the occasion, was left for Father, and the house stayed warm throughout the night.

❧

Two days later, Cyrille was woken by a sudden tug on his sleeve. It was Jean, in tears, scared and confused.

"He's back!" he yelled into his brother's ear. "He brought people from the town! They have torches!"

"What in God's name are you talking about?!" Shock and fear chased all the drowsiness from Cyrille's head.

"Sophie and Grandpa are talking to them now!" Jean yelled, and bolted through the door.

Cyrille rushed downstairs, almost breaking his ankle on the wooden steps. Mother was kneeling under a cross, deep in prayer, Mee at her side, tugging at her skirt with one hand, and picking at her teeth with the other. There was Jean crouching at the door, in tears. The door to the outside was open, and Cyrille saw Sophie's and Grandfather's backs. He pushed them aside as he emerged from the house.

There was a crowd of people waiting: residents of the town, people that he knew, people who mourned his father. Now those known and liked people, who—he thought—liked him and his family in return, were forming a semi-circle around the entrance to his house. They were all brandishing pitchforks, scythes, and torches, and their expressions were fearful and dumbfounded. And in the middle of that semi-circle stood Hugo Berger, the Bishop of Toulouse, now in full preacher's attire, with crimson furs and a gold cross on a chain.

"What's the meaning of this?!" Cyrille shouted, addressing the man who was obviously the author of this whole scene.

"They want to kill us!" yelled Sophie in helpless tears, embracing her brother. "Because of Father!"

"Even at your deathbed you won't let go of this sinful superstition!" Hugo Berger thundered, now in his full preacher voice.

Cyrille turned his gaze to the crowd, looking for a sympathetic face. Everyone looked away from him, contemplating the slushy dirty snow under their feet. No one spoke up, no one protested. It would be so easy for such a crowd to overpower a single man, but their fear was too great.

"Is that how you repay your saviors?!" Grandfather's lower lip shook stronger than ever before. "We helped you, fed you, and gave you a place to stay! And all of that doesn't matter because of our beliefs?!"

"Exactly!" Hugo Berger took a torch from a man standing closest to him. "Your deeds do not matter, when your beliefs are rotten! Feeding the dead is forbidden! And your parson confirmed that he has warned you on numerous occasions about that disgusting sin!"

Tears trickled down Sophie's cheeks. Every neighbor standing before her was aware that Father was still living with them. It was an unspoken rule to never discuss it, but she knew other families did it as well—they fed their dead siblings, spouses, parents, and kids. But it was the Guiscards who were caught in the act. And she knew there was no way for them to save themselves. She only hoped it wouldn't be as painful as she imagined.

On the clear order of the bishop, the villagers pushed all three of them into the house. Thick, rough cords were used to bind them all, each of the family members separately, even Mee, who burst into tears.

The doors were blocked from the outside and bundles of dry straw placed around the building to make the arson easier. Screams and cries meant nothing. Mrs. Guiscard begging for life of her youngest meant nothing.

Hugo Berger, the Bishop of Toulouse, made a sign of the cross and threw the first torch. Then the rest of the torches landed between the bunches of straw, and the fire grew in a matter of seconds, engulfing the whole house like a hungry beast.

The bishop engaged himself in a prayer, sometimes forgetting the words (he was never good at Latin), and making up some in his head. The roaring of the flames climbing the walls and licking the roof drowned out the shouting and crying. All the human sounds ceased quicker than Berger would expect. Perhaps the wretched animals were lucky and choked on the smoke. The pleasant smell of burning wood soon mixed with the sweeter smell of burning flesh.

After a while Berger got tired with reciting prayers, both real and made up. It's not like those peasants surrounding him could comprehend any of them or even distinguish between the real Latin and the fake. Besides, his throat began to hurt. He congratulated himself on a successful eradication of sin. He had a lot of such success before the scandal. Perhaps this one would help him clear his name.

That's what he pondered, standing before the house immersed in flames. The heat from the fire made him sweat—he stood way too close and the power of the flames was almost burning his own skin. That is why Berger thought it so peculiar when a wave of freezing cold shook his body. This feeling… He'd had it before… The sudden dread and realization he was no longer alone.

He sensed a presence behind his back. A distinct figure of a man about his height, though much thinner from the differences in diet. It was like the figure was made out of ice.

All of a sudden Berger's body shivered as if thrown into an ice-cold river. He stood before the burning house petrified, skin crawling and blood freezing. He heard a voice and somehow knew he was the only one who could hear it:

"All my life the nobility and the clergy took what was mine. My money, my horses, my cows, and finally, my life. And even when I'm dead, you cannot stop taking away all that I have!"

A cold hand rested on Berger's arm. It wasn't the cold of the winter—it was the cold of dead flesh. And the voice was now whispering into Berger's ear:

"I guess you'll be the one to feed me from now on."

SOMETHING

"THE BEST PLACE to hide is the green cupboard above the stove in the kitchen. Something never finds us there," Natalia said in her I-am-so-important voice. She put her hands on her hips and raised her head with the most condescending expression a six-year-old could have.

Mateusz disliked Natalia and yet listened to her. He was four years old, and his parents always told him to keep quiet and do what he was told. So he did. He always did what others told him to.

He hated being left with his cousins Natalia and Piotr. They always treated him terribly, bossing him around. If they played thieves and policemen, he was always the thief and he was always caught and jailed in the basement. If they played hunters and fox, Mateusz was given the role of the fox and at the end of the day was bruised all over from the little rubber balls shot at him from Piotr's toy gun. But the worst by far was playing house—Mateusz was the youngest, so it was only natural that he was the baby. And then he was given all sorts of nasty stuff to eat and sometimes, if he was "sick," real medicine from the first aid cabinet.

If Mateusz was ever encouraged to ask questions, he would ponder why Piotr ever put up with his older sister—there was only a year gap between the two, but following her orders all day must've been annoying. Possibly, he would've noticed that Piotr liked to gang up on him with Natalia, but had his own share of bruises from fights with her. It was only when Mateusz was visiting the two worked in cahoots.

On this occasion Mateusz was to spend the evening and the entire night with his cousins. Neither his parents nor his aunt believed in hiring nannies or asking neighbors to take care of their children during their outings. They instead believed three kids would be perfectly capable of taking care of themselves, as long as they threatened them enough into obedience.

So before Mom, Dad, and Auntie left, Mateusz and his cousins were told to go to sleep right after the evening children's program on TV. They were also told they could only eat cookies if they ate dinner first, and that there better be no destruction in the house or they wouldn't feel their asses the next day.

Soon after the adults left, the dinner was dumped into the toilet. It was a tasteless, overcooked slush of groats, that could've been saved with some salt and a lot of straining, but no child would prefer it over cookies. And it wasn't every day they got a whole packet to themselves. The cheap, sugar-coated cookies were one of the two good things that happened to Mateusz that day.

The second was the bedtime show on TV. The only part of the day when all three sat quietly next to each other, munching on cookies, and watching Little Mole take care of an orphaned eagle chick.

And then it started. A single bang from upstairs made all three of them jump up. Piotr and Natalia perked up their ears, freezing in place in complete silence. The bang sounded like a piece of furniture falling over, but no other sound followed.

"It's not coming down yet," whispered Natalia to her brother.

"What's coming down?" Mateusz whispered back, terrified.

"It's **not**. It's **not** coming down," Piotr hissed at him in annoyance, and added in a threatening voice, "At least for now."

"Something appears upstairs and comes down to look for us when Mommy's not home," Natalia explained, keeping her voice down, a little above a whisper. "It sniffs loudly and growls. I think it wants to eat us!"

"Why?"

"Because it's hungry, stupid! Monsters eat children when they're hungry!"

"And what did Auntie Sandra say?" asked Mateusz.

"What?" Natalia cowered slightly.

"What did Auntie say? Does she know how to kill the monster?"

"We never talk to Mommy about silly things like a big old monster! We know how to hide from it!" Natalia snapped at Mateusz and quickly turned her back on the boys to wipe the tears that formed tiny droplets in the corners of her eyes.

The truth was that Natalia did tell her mom about Something.

The morning after Something's very first appearance , the moment she heard the key turning in the lock of the entrance door, Natalia rushed downstairs to embrace her mother. With tears in her eyes, she described a horrifying beast that roamed the house, sniffing and snarling.

Through the fumes of digested alcohol, her mother told her to stop bothering her with idiotic stories. Natalia insisted, clinging to Mother's skirt so tightly she made her stumble. Sandra bumped her head on a doorframe, which caused her head, already heavy with booze, to erupt in a splitting headache. And Natalia was given the whooping of her life. That was the first and last time Natalia said anything about Something to her mother.

"So where should we hide?" asked Mateusz.

Hearing that, Piotr scoffed, and Natalia turned on her patronizing tone and told Mateusz about the green cupboard above the stove.

"C-can I hide with you?" Mateusz had already anticipated the answer so his throat was tight with incoming tears.

"No way!" exclaimed Piotr with sadistic satisfaction.

"Obviously not, duh!" added Natalia. "The cupboard is **our** hideout! Find your own!"

And there it was—full-on tears, hot, and rolling down Mateusz's cheeks in streams.

"You're always mean to me!"

"Quit your whining! The cupboard isn't big enough for all three of us anyways!"

"I bet there's no monster! You just want to scare me!" Mateusz yelled between sobs.

That insult could not be left unpunished. Natalia's cheeks turned red from anger.

"There **is** a monster! Do not call me a liar, you little shit!" Recently Natalia's mother had started to call her that, and Natalia finally found an occasion to use that phrase. She was ready to punch Mateusz, so he could learn his place, but she was interrupted by another sudden noise from upstairs.

Upstairs Something growled angrily. The second they heard it, they froze in place. Even Mateusz ceased crying.

A long hoarse sigh made their blood run cold. There was no doubt now—Something was upstairs.

Piotr and Natalia bolted before Mateusz managed to blink. He heard rustling and stomping in the kitchen as his cousins climbed the stove and shut the door.

Another snarl from upstairs. And a thump. Then another. Stomping. Something was moving toward the stairs.

The steps were slow and deliberate, almost like they were intended as a warning that the monster was coming. Another hoarse sigh made Mateusz's skin crawl. He bolted toward the door and realized in panic that he found himself in the hall. Right next to the staircase.

Mateusz saw it—at the top of the stairs—a huge hairy paw with claws as long as half his arm rested on the banister. One of the claws tapped impatiently on the wood. The rest of the body was hidden behind the wall.

And then instinct kicked in. The instinct that made millions of young of millions of species survive since the beginning of life.

In the hall there was a small round table covered with a cloth so long it reached the floor. Mateusz dove under it and cowered, making sure his arms and legs weren't sticking out. The cloth had lace at its edges, so Mateusz saw what descended the stairs.

It walked on two legs, and it walked slowly, wheezing with effort. Every step down was a scratch of the talons on the tiles. Front legs were folded like the legs of a velociraptor. They outstretched every so often to tap on the walls and furniture with their long, curved claws.

Something stepped in front of him. It sniffed around and then…

KNOCK! KNOCK!

Something tapped its claw on the table surface. Mateusz uttered a weak squeal before clasping his hands on his mouth. Something snarled in surprise. Mateusz could see it slowly bending over the table and smelling frantically. And finally…

The huge snout dug its way under the tablecloth. The nostrils expanded with a loud long whiz. Mateusz bit his fingers, forcing himself to stay quiet, the beast's nose almost touching his face. Tears rolled down his cheeks, but he would not move, would not make a sound.

The last whiff of air, an annoyed growl, and the snout backed out. Huge claws clicked on the tile floor when Something straightened itself up. And it moved on.

Mateusz shook violently, hearing the snout sniffing and the claws drumming on furniture. It walked into Natalia and Piotr's bedroom and then into the dining room. The claws drummed on the TV, and a box of cookies crunched under Something's foot. It snarled as if in realization and returned to the hall, walking much faster than previously. Mateusz curled into a ball, hiding his head between his knees, certain that Something was coming for him. But it walked right into the kitchen.

Now the sniffing intensified. The claws drummed on the kitchen table, on the fridge, on the sink. He heard the squeak of the oven door being opened and the rattling of metal plates inside. He heard a faint, fearful squeal. And then he heard the cupboard door fly open. The high-pitched screams of his cousins and the roar of the beast pierced his ears and drilled itself into his brain.

He lost consciousness.

Before he fully woke, some new sounds entered his brain. He didn't understand them at first, though they seemed familiar. He wanted to ignore them, but they insisted, louder and angrier each time. And then he woke up—under the table in the hall, his pants uncomfortably wet.

"Mateusz! Piotr?! Natalia!" he heard a mixture of three voices and frantic footsteps all around the house. Auntie! And Mom and Dad! They were back!

He shot from under the table right into his mother's embrace. He hugged her like he never had before. The faint smell of cheap perfume, and the smell of vodka on her breath and her dress (because someone spilled a drink on her) was somehow the most beautiful combination of scents in the world. Mom hugged him back, but without much enthusiasm—she was tired and irritated.

"They're playing hide and seek!" she informed her husband and sister with a sigh.

"Oh, for God's sake!" Auntie came down the stairs, her heels clicking unpleasantly on the tiles. She always spoke with a slight slurp, but after libation it was even more prominent. "Where are those two?!"

"The green cupboard," replied Mateusz in a weak whisper.

"What?!"

"The green cupboard, above the stove."

In a few heavy clicking steps, Auntie entered the kitchen. With fury, she threw open the cupboard door and shrieked in terror. She stumbled back, bumped into the kitchen table, and held her hand to her heart, hyperventilating.

"What is this?! What the fuck is this?!" She pointed at the opened cupboard, nearly fainting.

Mateusz's parents rushed into the kitchen. And when they saw what was inside the cupboard, they froze, faces pale with horror.

"Is it...?" Mateusz's mother said softly.

"Blood," confirmed her husband. "Sandra, your kids have a sick sense of humor."

"They don't know how to write yet, you idiot!" Auntie yelled back, slowly slipping onto a chair, clutching her left breast, her heart pounding.

"Something was here," Mateusz tried to explain politely.

"What was here?" His father frowned.

"Someone came here and did this?!" Auntie wheezed and coughed. "Police! We need the police!"

With these words, Auntie marched out of the kitchen to the dining room, where the phone was. Mateusz's parents stayed in the kitchen, staring intensely at the open cupboard. Climbing on his toes, Mateusz could see the letters scribbled inside the empty cupboard. And if he could read, he would know they formed the words:

THIS TIME I FOUND THEM

THE WHITE CAT

IT WAS WHITE with blue eyes and meowing in terror, as one of the boys approached it with a knife in his hand.

"Gasoline is better," said another boy, showing the bottle to his comrades.

"I have a match!" shouted another enthusiastically, reaching into his pocket.

The cat's eyes grew larger and darker. There was no way of escaping from three huge creatures surrounding it. It could sense their intentions were not friendly.

As the punk struggled with the cap of the gasoline bottle, a pebble flew through the air. It was a small thing, but became a formidable weapon once given speed by launching it with a strong arm. And Camila, though only sixteen years of age, was surprisingly strong.

A short exclamation of pain and surprise tore the air, as the pebble hit the boy's forearm, knocking the bottle out of his hand.

"Get away from it, you beasts!" Camila was older and taller than the three boys gathered around a defenseless cat. She was armed with a handful of pebbles and a large wicker grocery basket. She was also furious.

"Ow! What's your problem, you stupid—?!" he didn't finish his cuss, as another pebble cut the skin on his bare calf.

"Beat it! Before I tell your fathers on you!"

At the sound of this threat all the boys turned pale. A moment later all that was left in the back alley was Camila, the cat, and a cloud of dust.

The cat's muscles relaxed just a little at the sight of its attackers running. But there was still Camila, and the cat wasn't about to trust any human being. It hissed when she reached out to it, and Camila had to back up to avoid being scratched.

Her heart almost broke at the sight of the wretched creature. Its fur was certainly snow white under the layers of dried-up mud. Pus was building in the corners of its eyes. Tiny cuts and scabs were a dubious decoration of its paws and face.

"It's all right. I want to help you," she said, reaching out to it once more. Her hand moved slowly, palm up to show that she wasn't holding any weapon. This time the cat sniffed her hand and rubbed its face against her fingers.

Camila picked it up gently and placed it in her wicker grocery basket—there was a lot of free space in it. Camila never had enough money to fill it, but it was the only thing she had to carry her meagre groceries. Right then the basket included some potatoes and a single celery stalk.

"I live not far from here," she said to the cat, directing her steps out of the back alley. The main street didn't look much better than the side streets—it wasn't dirty, but it was humble. And pretty empty, as most of its residents were currently at the market or working at the docks.

Not five minutes later she reached her flat. It consisted of two rooms on the second floor of one of the many run-down houses by the river. The first room served as a kitchen, a washroom, and a bedroom. The entrance to the second room was covered with a grey blanket. Still, her accommodation was way better than many others like it along the river; there was no mold. Also, Camila claimed, they had the best view in town.

"It's not much, but it's safe. And you are more than welcome to stay as long as you like."

The floorboards creaked as Camila stepped on them. She put the basket on the floor as there was no table in the room. The cat was quite relaxed by then and sniffed at its new surroundings, safely sitting among potatoes.

"Adele's usually still asleep at this hour," said Camila softly. "Let's not wake her. Sleep is the only relief she still has." The cat looked at her as if taking in the information. It had such wise, understanding eyes, much like Adele's.

Camila took a small basin, poured in the water from the kettle, still warm as she prepared some water for her own wash just a half an hour before. She chose a clean piece of cloth, soaked it in warm water, and started to clean the mud from the cat.

The creature was peaceful and obedient. It squinted its eyes, focusing on the sensation of warmth soothing its body. And Camila marveled at how beautiful the animal was under the cover of dirt. So funny! Such a perfectly functioning body, a core that could live for years and years, enjoying perfect health and clear senses. And all of that for such a small, insignificant creature. And then there was Adele, slowly driven out of her own body amidst excruciating pain.

"Wouldn't it be nice to just change your body if the old one is used-up and tired?" she asked, washing the pus away from the cat's eyes. "Why should you cease to exist only because the flesh you walk in decays?" She quickly wiped a tear from her cheek. "I'm just making myself cry. I'm such an idiot!"

"Caaamilaaa!" The weak moan from the other room startled the cat.

"That's Adele," Camila said, rising to her feet. The bath was finished anyway.

The cat followed her to the second room, beyond the grey blanket. The air there was stiff (the only window wasn't opening) and pungent with the smell of unrest and suffering. A bed was the only piece of furniture in there, and on the bed lay Adele, contorted amongst sheets soaked in her sweat.

"I'm sorry," Adele whispered hoarsely as her sister sat on the edge of the mattress. "I made a mess."

Indeed, a fresh blood stain was slowly drying on the pillow. Over the past few days Adele had been coughing more frequently.

"You don't have to apologize, silly," Camila swiftly exchanged the dirty pillow for a folded-up blanket. "I'll wash it right away."

Not wanting to waste words, Adele smiled faintly and nodded. If speaking wasn't necessary, she didn't speak—her body hurt less that way.

Adele was the kind of a person that hated to be a bother. And according to her, she had been nothing but a bother for weeks.

Camila was about to ask her sister if she wanted breakfast, when the cat jumped onto the bed.

"Oh!" sighed Adele in delighted surprise; she'd always loved animals.

"We have a new tenant," Camila said. Her sister nodded and almost smiled. The cat, now completely calm, sniffed at Adele's face—there was still some blood at the corner of her mouth. Adele raised her withered hand to stroke it, and it let her. It even started to purr, lying next to her chest.

Camila brought her sister breakfast, and while feeding her, she told her about how she rescued the poor creature from the hooligans. Adele listened patiently, swallowing boiled oatmeal. And as soon as she was finished, she fell asleep again.

Camila fixed her gaze on her sister's face, tears building up under her eyelids. It was the third day in a row Adele only woke to eat or relieve herself. She suspected it wouldn't be much longer before…

She quickly stood, took the dirty pillow and the dirty bowl, and marched out of the room, leaving the cat by her sister's side.

She ate her own oatmeal, washed the bloodied pillow, and went to her usual job. People around town would bring her their clothes to mend and wash, earning her a few pennies here and there. After she finished, she went out to deliver the fixed clothes. She came back with several sheets to wash and stitch up. In the meantime she made dinner (a thin potato soup with a stalk of celery to hopefully add some flavor). It was then the cat decided to leave Adele's side and come to eat. It enthusiastically lapped up the soup left for it in a shallow tin, and went right back into Adele's room.

Adele woke in the late afternoon. Camila gave her the soup and helped her relieve herself. After that Adele fell asleep again.

It's good that she sleeps, thought Camila, and tears trickled freely down her cheeks. *She's in much less pain that way.* Choking on her tears, Camila left the room again.

As evening came, and there wasn't enough light in the room to work, Camila sat by the windowsill and opened the kitchen window. She looked upon the setting sun, slowly diving behind the buildings on the other side of the river. She observed the boats on the river and the colors of the sunset reflected in the water. There were noisy kids skipping stones. Gulls screamed annoyingly at each other. The barking of a dog; the laughter of a couple; the impatient nagging of an elderly woman. There was so much life around! And everything and everyone would continue living the next day. There would be tomorrow for them. Would there be tomorrow for Adele? And if yes, would that be a good thing?

The meowing of the cat snapped her out of her meditation. Camila's face was red and slick from tears. At first her heart skipped a beat, as she was certain the cat wanted to inform her…

She heard a moan from the other room—the kind of moan Adele made in her sleep. *No. Not yet.* Camila sighed in relief, and addressed the cat angrily, "You have nine lives, why don't you lend one to Adele?"

The cat meowed again. It was hungry, but Camila didn't have anything to give it. She had a few pennies from her work that day. She'd go to the market first thing in the morning.

"Go away!" she hissed at it quietly so she didn't wake Adele. First, the cat cocked its head as if to ponder what the person before him meant to communicate. And then, as if it was never interested in getting anything from her, it went back to Adele's bedroom to watch over her.

That night Camila cried herself to sleep.

❧

A beam of sunlight shining straight at her face woke her up. The riverbanks outside her window were already buzzing with activity. She heard barges' bells and people shouting greetings from their boats. She heard seagulls, and dogs, and even a cow that someone must've been bringing to the market. But inside her little apartment there was silence, and stillness so complete, it could mean only one thing.

Her blood ran cold. Slowly, she turned to the grey blanket hanging in the doorway between two rooms. Stepping softly, Camila approached Adele's bedroom. She pulled the blanket aside and looked inside.

The cat was sitting next to Adele's face. It pawed at it gently, trying to figure something out. Adele's skin was deathly white. Every sleeping body has its own little movements: the chest rising and dropping, eyelids quivering, nostrils inhaling and exhaling. There was nothing. That body was as still as a stone figure.

Camila came closer and outstretched her arm, her shaking fingertips touching Adele's cheek. She didn't know a human body could be this cold. She dropped on her knees.

She moaned and howled for what seemed like hours. Tears

ran down her cheeks in two hot streams. She choked on her cries, banging on the floor with her closed fists. She rolled onto her back and yelled until her throat gave out. And finally, when she raised herself up from the floor to look at her sister once again, she realized the cat was still sitting there, at Adele's head.

It cocked its head at her and spoke, "Camila, please! That is enough!"

The voice was unmistakable.

"Adele?" she whimpered, barely forcing a sound from her tired throat.

"It took me a while to make the cat speak. But I'm here, sweetie. This body doesn't hurt at all!"

"H-how?" Camila's head spun.

"It saw my suffering and decided to lend me some space inside it. We're here together. The cat says it'll let me take over for now—it wants to sleep anyway."

"It's really you!" Camila stood and snatched the cat into her arms. She hugged it long and tight, way too tight for the delicate animal. It was uncomfortable and meowed pleadingly to be let go. But Camila wouldn't; she held it for the next hour.

"I'm so happy! I saved that cat just in time!"

At Adele's funeral Camila seemed more bored than grieving. Some people said that she smiled when her sister's body was lowered into the hole in the ground. And she was the first to leave the cemetery, avoiding everyone who tried to give her their condolences.

"Poor girl must be in shock," commented the butcher's wife the next day. "Her sister was the last person she had left, and now she's all alone."

"She didn't even cry! Not a single tear! It's monstrous!" insisted one of the washerwomen.

"She surely cried enough before the funeral," the barber

advised everyone who came to his shop. "She simply has nothing left."

"She's carrying that white cat around all day! All day!" whispered one scullery maid to another.

"Not all day, only when she goes outside. She carries it in that wicker basket of hers."

"And she talks to it constantly. And pauses as if the cat is responding!"

"Do you think she's gone crazy?"

"She could, after what happened to her…"

"Completely crazy!"

"She's just dealing with loneliness, that's all."

"She should be locked up!"

"And do you know what else? Wait till you hear!"

"Do you know what she named the cat?"

"A stupid cat! Her sister must be rolling in her grave!"

"She calls the cat 'Adele!'"

SLEEPLESS TRUTH

It was unusual for Katherine Davis to receive a call from work at four in the morning. She was understandably annoyed, but her contract stated that she had to be available 24/7, so she had no choice but to follow the orders she received.

Exactly fifty-five minutes later she boarded the helicopter sent for her to the nearest airport. Her boss was already there. He handed her the file containing all the data the office had managed to gather. By that time she was fully awake and her initial irritation turned into curiousness.

"Why the short notice?" she asked Emmerson via the microphone attached to her noise-cancelling headphones.

"There's a serious risk the guy you're about to interview will either die or attempt to kill himself. He's under constant supervision, of course, and he **seems** to be in a good shape… But…"

"Buuut?"

"Just read the damn papers, Davis! I'm not a morning person," scoffed Emmerson, popping a strip of chewing gum into his mouth.

Working for the FBI as a cult specialist with PhDs in both psychology and sociology meant a lot of out-of-the-norm requests. Still, Katherine's job consisted mostly of familiarizing herself with tons of paperwork and giving her opinion to the bureau. The

FBI needed her to evaluate hundreds of new cults popping up all around the US each year. About 98% of them were completely harmless (except for scamming naïve people out of their money), but once in a while something more sinister emerged. She was the one to tell the boys in suits who to watch out for, like potential terrorists or suicide cults. She took pride in being almost 100% accurate in her predictions, and the bureau paid well for her expertise. The popular opinion was that if she was alive at the time, Jonestown would never have happened.

She was still young, and the job hadn't taken its toll on her psyche yet, despite all the depravity she'd already witnessed: sites of mass suicides, teenage girls forced to "give themselves up" to cult leaders, kids tortured to punish their parents. All the sewage of the human condition pouring through the deeds and words of gullible fanatics.

And yet those stories taking the first pages of newspapers and prime time on television were just a tiny slice of reality. An exception, not the norm. Most cults disappeared within two years of their establishment. Most of them sold remedies to all of life's problems or the life eternal on the other side. Most of the cults existed because their founders wanted money, and nothing sells better than salvation.

And there was The Temple of Heavenly Peace.

Adorable name—infantile and megalomaniacal at the same time. They started as an addiction center, focusing on drug and alcohol addictions. *Sounds great!* The founder of the center promoted his own alternative methods… *Red alert! Red alert!* The method was replacing the high created by drugs and alcohol with a high created by sleep deprivation. Then the system of initiations and "higher truths" was created. Sleep was sinful and unnatural, another outcome of the original sin. Hence, for the people to purge themselves of their sinful nature, they had to cleanse themselves from the need of sleep. That was the return to the pure, original state of the human condition.

The Temple cleverly interpreted actual effects of sleep deprivation. After twenty-four hours without sleep a person becomes irritable and drowsy. The Temple claimed it was the evil and laziness "pouring out." After seventy-two hours of sleep deprivation people experience hallucinations—according to The Temple the demons gathered around to taunt them and force them to go back to sleep.

Of course prolonged sleep deprivation is harmful on both physical and psychological levels. The effects include increased heart rate, high blood pressure, attention deficit, short-term memory loss, mood swings, fatigue, anxiety, paranoia, and impulsive behavior. Your immune system is a shambles, your sex drive is gone, your balance and coordination suffer, you gain weight and increase your chance for type 2 diabetes. The good news is that even after prolonged sleep deprivation your body can easily go back to a normal sleep-wake cycle and repair most of the damage. If it's allowed to…

The unraveling of The Temple of Heavenly Peace started with an accident on 1st and Roosevelt at 11:42 p.m. when a car drove straight into a shop window. The woman driving the vehicle had a displaced kneecap and a broken wrist, but seemed not to feel any pain. She tried to walk out of the car, babbling something about a rat living with her. At the hospital she was tested for drugs, but the results were negative.

The police questioned her, and with a quivering lip she asked for her purse. From it she produced a notebook and pointed at one of the addresses, claiming she needed to be there by 7 p.m., or else she'd go to hell. The policemen decided not to enlighten her about the actual hour of the day, afraid the lady would lose it. They also learned the woman had been awake for four days as a way of cleansing herself from demons. When the police interview was over, the hospital staff tried to put the woman to sleep. That made her hysterical, yelling that if she went to sleep the rat living in her stomach would divorce her.

At 1:12 a.m. six policemen raided flat 1C in the apartment complex on Cedar Street. Apartment 1C's main room had been turned into what seemed like a cell from a psychiatric ward—locked from the outside and the door had a hatch to serve meals. Inside there was no furniture, the walls and the floor were padded with mattresses, and the only window was boarded up. The light from the ceiling lamp was so extremely bright it blinded the officers who opened the room.

One man, beaten to a pulp, lay unconscious close to the door, face down. A woman with a black eye and fat lip cowered at the wall farthest from the entrance. And there was a second man, sitting right next to the door, smoking a cigarette. He had some bruises on his neck and face, and a shirt with a torn-off pocket and a partially ripped out collar.

When the police entered the room, the woman sitting opposite them fainted. And the smoking man smothered the cigarette butt on the floor and said, "Good you're here. We can end this circus."

"Austin Klein is the one you're gonna interview. He's currently facing murder charges for Brian Mahoney, the guy he beat up. Mahoney died in the ambulance," said Emmerson when Katherine raised her head from above the papers.

"Did he say why he did it?"

"Yeah. They were there to help each other stay awake. Austin is apparently Temple's expert on the matter. He testified that during those "purification sessions" physical torture is the norm. They'd apparently been sitting there for two days, and the woman, Rebecca Webb, was taking it pretty bad. Allegedly, Austin refused to hurt her in any way, so Brian was the one to administer the beatings. When he started to kick her in the stomach, Austin drew the line. The fight between the two ensued. Brian lost."

"It says the door was locked from the outside. Was anybody else there?"

"Yes, but they escaped through the window when they heard the sirens. Austin gave a name, but has no idea where the guy lives."

Katherine flipped the papers. She was looking at Klein's file, and as she read, her eyes grew wide.

"No fucking way!" she exclaimed and instantly covered her mouth. Her New Year's resolution was to stop cursing.

"What?" Emmerson turned to her.

"Klein says that he's been awake since October 12th! That's over four months! The known record of sleep deprivation is eleven days. That would be... I cannot even imagine what would happen to him if he really..."

"I was advised that he's in perfect health. His blood pressure's not even elevated."

"He must be lying."

"Most likely. But he's still the best shot we have to learn more about The Temple."

"Temple's not registered, is it?"

"No."

"The leader?"

"On the run. The boys are tracking him as we speak. He must've learned about the police busting one of his minion's torture sessions."

"Other members?"

"Austin gave some names, but the members were instructed not to disclose their addresses to each other. He knew the address we found him under and that's it."

Katherine took a good long look at her boss. She closed the file and put it neatly on the seat next to her.

"So why am I here, Jack? It seems this Klein guy hides nothing, and he's been interrogated already."

"We need a deep-dive analysis, Katherine. For a guy who's supposed to be sleep-deprived, he's strangely coherent. I was warned that he seemed to be having hallucinations, and yet he's cool as a cucumber. He's also perfectly fine with spending the rest of his life in prison for murder."

"He wouldn't be the first."

"Let's just do our job, Katherine," Emmerson snapped, irritated. So she shut up, knowing her boss reacted like that when he himself wasn't sure what his supervisors wanted to achieve.

ꟹ

Ninety minutes later they were riding the bureau's car to the office. Only seven minutes after their landing, Emmerson got a call on his cell.

"Yeah? Just now?… Alright." He ended the call and turned to Katherine. "Rebecca Webb died of internal injuries."

"Should I threaten Klein with pinning that death on him if he's not talkative enough?" she joked ironically.

"You can threaten him with your mother-in-law's cooking, if it gets the job done."

Both Jack and Katherine chortled.

After a while of silence, Emmerson spoke again, more softly, and with much more pain in his voice. "Why do people have to die because of some stupid-shit beliefs? Can you explain it to me?"

"To you their beliefs are bullshit, but to them they may be worth dying for. And sometimes death is just human stupidity added to unfortunate circumstances."

ꟹ

Austin Klein was very much an average man. Not handsome, not ugly, medium build, medium height, thirty-two years old. Earned good money at a car dealership, lived alone, had a social life, liked to jog, had a pet chinchilla. Average.

The moment Katherine was let into the interrogation room, Austin put down his cigarette. She tilted her head down to appear unintimidating and help her interlocutor let his guard down. But she kept him at the edge of her vision.

Austin looked at her right side first, straight to her right, as if something of importance was there. Only after that he looked at Katherine. She noticed his lips curling into a polite smile, which disappeared almost instantly. He must've thought this wasn't an appropriate occasion to smile. She introduced herself, and he introduced himself back, and on the same breath of air he asked, "Do you know how she is?"

Now Katherine shot her head up, honestly not understanding the question.

"Rebecca," Austin prompted her.

She put her papers down and straightened herself on the chair, fingers of both hands interlocked.

"I'm sorry," she said delicately.

Austin slanted himself against the chair's backrest and exhaled sharply.

"Those fuckers turn you into a brainless puppet!" He jerked a slightly crushed cigarette from his packet and popped it between his lips. "I'm sorry. Can I smoke?" He turned to her.

After Katherine nodded, and after the nose-drilling stench of tobacco soared to the ventilation system, she asked, "Why did you say they turn you into a brainless puppet?"

"Because they do!" Austin bent toward her and spoke faster and faster, picking up pace with each sentence. "I've seen so many people physically abused during those sessions! Very little fazed me anymore, you know? I should've reacted sooner! The very moment Brian forced Rebecca onto the floor. But I watched when he kicked her the first time, and the second, and the third! I sat there like a braindead zombie, gawking at a psychologically unstable prick killing a woman! It took me a while to understand what was happening and to kick his ass."

"He died too, you know," Katherine forced her tone to be indifferent.

Austin laughed a short, gurgling laugh. "He doesn't fuck up my karma."

"And Rebecca's death does?"

"No. That's on Brian. Because I tried to help her, I got some points."

Alright, thought Katherine, *Possible PTSD on top of sleep deprivation.*

She changed her position in the chair, crossing her legs. She smacked her lips and sighed loudly to give herself the appearance of a woman at a loss.

"I usually talk to complete devotees of their cults, but you seem to be a skeptic."

Austin exhaled a puff of smoke through his nose, chuckling. "I'm not a skeptic, lady. I'm their antichrist! The reason I was still attending those sessions was that Murray… Sorry… **The High Shephard** was too stupid to understand that! When I began refusing to take part in purifications, he started to pay me! And wanted me to talk as much as possible about my 'visions.' He believed they were good for his little flock of sheep."

"And what are those 'visions'?" she asked.

That question broke something within Austin. His face, up to that point contorted with anger and frustration, relaxed into a solemn sulk. The man crushed the cigarette butt in the ashtray with a gloomy expression on his face.

"Did you see something on my right when I walked in?" she asked softly. Instinctively, Austin looked to her right again and quickly back down.

"Yeah," he replied, drawing circles in the ash with the cigarette butt.

"Can you tell me about it?"

Austin kept silent and kept drawing.

"Let's imagine that whatever you tell me, I'm going to believe you," she said with a smug smile.

Austin's pupils grew larger and he burst out laughing. "I like you, lady! You know your shrink bullshit. And you also know when to drop it." He lit another cigarette and attempted to rock in his chair. The chair was screwed to the floor, and Austin himself was chained to the desk, which he seemed not to have noticed before. So instead of rocking, he lay his chest on the table, tucking his arms under it, licked his lip and said, "Okay, lady, I'll tell you! But you'll be sorry you took this job."

Yeah, never heard that one before, she thought, slightly vexed.

"I call them Companions. They're vaguely humanoid with very few facial features. And each human being has their own.

"First, I was sure I saw demons. That was when I still believed in Murray's lies. Their appearances change depending on the bad and good deeds of the person they accompany. That's why I know I can trust you," Austin pointed to Katherine's right. "Yours isn't that bad."

"That's good, right?" she smiled encouragingly.

"Yeah, if I were you, I wouldn't change." He puffed out the smoke and flicked some ash off the cigarette's burning end.

"When did you start seeing them?"

"Not before my third week awake. The first was my own, right in the mirror next to me. I thought I'd fucking die!" Austin took a good, long look at his right. "Funny thing is, it looked surprised that I can see it. Must not happen too often…

"Because The Temple encourages sharing, I confessed my visions to the rest. Many, many exorcisms later…" Austin paused to laugh heartily for about two minutes. "…Many exorcisms later, I began seeing other people's Companions. I wasn't sleeping all that time, so I guess it was a natural progression of my 'visions.'

"Anyway, when I began seeing other people's Companions, I shared that revelation as well. So Murray decided every person has their own guardian angel that turns ugly because of the sins that person commits. I've become somewhat of a celebrity in The Temple."

"So you see them all the time now?" Katherine asked and Austin nodded.

"When I finally saw Murray's Companion," Austin chortled again, "he changed his mind and decided that I don't see guardian angels but demons. The more pious and righteous a person, the uglier the demon gets, because it needs to be stronger to successfully tempt them."

"Murray must have had a really ugly one." Katherine smiled as Austin shook from uncontrollable laughter.

"Motherfucker could kill with its looks!!"

She needed to wait for Klein to calm down. And it took a while, since Austin's laughter was close to hysterical. She began to wonder if she should call someone, because it started to look like a seizure. Thankfully, that's when Austin stopped. Tears were running down his cheeks, but he wasn't smiling anymore.

"Perhaps it wouldn't be that bad if I hadn't seen that one death," he sniffed loudly. "During the purification session. At that time I was still a believer. They were constantly asking me to join different sessions—I was to be an example to encourage other people to make the effort."

Austin sniffed again, crushed another cigarette butt in the ashtray, and lit another right away. The stench of tobacco made Katherine sick to her stomach, but she was tough enough to hold it in. Austin's confessions were now of the utmost importance, and if they needed cigarette smoke to come out, so be it!

"His name was Randall. He was twenty, maybe twenty-one. Alcoholic from a broken home. Somehow he was one of the most decent people I've ever met. He got addicted when he was ten—his precious father saw to it.

"I talked with that kid for hours. He was a good person. Not malicious, not evil. But he had no education, and couldn't hold down a job because of his addiction. And he..."

Austin's voice shuddered and broke down. Katherine, who hadn't been looking at him for a while, believing that would make his confessions flow smoother, raised her head. She saw a shivering man, with tears running down his cheeks in streams.

"His body gave out the same night. He had a heart attack. He died right next to me and I saw his Companion... Oh, God!"

Austin hid his face in his hands. When he spoke again, his voice was high-pitched. That's how strongly his throat had tightened.

"Every depiction of hell ever created is true! Only you are not thrown into some fiery pit. It happens right here, right after you die." Austin sobbed and took several tissues from the box standing on the table.

"I think," he continued when he was able to speak again. "I think these things are parasites. I think they're sadistic, and they love torturing us, but they can only get to your soul when you're dead. And then it starts. The worse a person is during their lifetime, the nastier their Companion gets after it can finally reach them. Randall... I saw his intestines spilling, his muscles tearing apart fiber by fiber! His eyes gouged out... The way he screamed, before his tongue... How can anyone...? God!

"And from that time on I saw it again and again. Randomly, I see a soul and its torturer. Out in the streets, in my own home, at my office! Anywhere! They called me a suicide risk." Austin raised his arm to show her the chains binding him to the desk. "How could anyone commit suicide when they know what awaits them on the other side?"

He sobbed and whimpered uncontrollably, again dangerously close to hysteria. Katherine decided to intervene.

"I'm certain that you saw many terrible things. But please, be aware that after seventy-two hours of sleep deprivation hallucinations start. If you haven't slept since October 12th, you are the most sleep-deprived person on record. No wonder your hallucinations seem so real."

"You… think… those are… hallucinations?" Austin was now hyperventilating.

"I know so! Hallucinations can happen to anyone, but hallucination's content, the 'what' of your hallucinations, is determined by your cultural environment. Surely you've encountered numerous depictions of hell throughout your life, haven't you?"

Austin nodded, shaking violently.

"You've been forever impacted by the gruesome and visceral depictions of after-life torment. Sleep deprivation is also tightly aligned with anxiety and paranoia. Obviously you see terrible things. But they're not real!"

"They're not real," he echoed her in a whisper.

"We're gonna help you. And we'll start with putting you to bed."

"That won't work," he sniveled in a more collected voice.

"Why not?"

"You think I haven't tried to go back to sleep? I've tried every method possible! I exhausted myself, I meditated, I took prescription drugs, I numbed myself with alcohol and weed. Nothing helps! I cannot sleep!"

"We shall see about that," Katherine replied in a confident tone. "When we put you to sleep, you'll probably awake naturally after several days, so we need to finish here first…"

"I think that sleep is a sort of a sedative," Austin said, completely ignoring her. "Insects inject their prey with anticoagulants, digestive juices and such to prepare it for eating. Companions numb us with sleep so we cannot see them. If we saw them, we would no longer reproduce and they would no longer be able to feed."

"Did any other member of The Temple have the same hallucinations as you do?" She ignored him back, trying to steer the conversation away from the topics that upset him.

"Nobody managed to stay awake long enough," said Austin, hanging his head.

"Your co-member was certain there was a rat about to divorce her," Katherine informed him, continuing her efforts to reason with his trauma. "See how silly—?"

"Terry's gay."

Katherine froze. She was expecting Austin to start spewing irrelevant, disjointed sentences at some point. In fact, she was impressed she hadn't heard them so far. But this. There was a problem with this sentence.

"What did you say?" For a second she lost her composure and it came out sounding confrontational.

"That your brother is gay. Don't sound so shocked, you knew already." Austin's chin rested on his chest, and his bangs obscured his face. In such a position his voice should have difficulties getting out, but it was booming...

"He only told you. And his boyfriend knows, of course. It's not like he could ever tell that to your homophobic asshole of a father. You call your father an asshole sometimes, don't you? You mumble when you're doing your makeup."

At first she thought she'd been had. This guy was a hired actor, they forced her to get out of bed at 4 a.m., and they planned to... What? Her birthday was in two months. A promotion? A cruel joke? Was she drugged? What?

If Austin said something about the barbecue when her dress tore and half her family saw her left buttock, or the fishing trip when her neighbor Joshua kissed her drunkenly, everything would be easy. She wasn't the only one who knew about those. But Terry?! She'd never told anyone, not even her husband!

She turned to the one-way mirror and mouthed, "What the fuck?" expecting some sort of answer. That answer did not come.

"Also," Austin continued. "When they woke you this morning, you sneaked into Ashley's room. You wanted a quick breakfast, and

Ashley often forgets the sandwiches you make for her and leaves them in her backpack. You found a sandwich, and you found a packet of cigarettes."

For the first time in her life Katherine was sure she was going to pass out. She searched frantically in her mind for a possible explanation for this phenomena. How could anyone know? She'd left the cigarettes in Ashley's backpack and told nobody. Her husband, awoken by the phone call, was back to sleep by then.

"Don't be too harsh on her," said Austin. "The cigarettes aren't hers. Jess smokes and needed to hide her stash, Ashley agreed. She didn't even try to smoke."

Katherine realized tears were rolling down her cheeks. There was no possible explanation, unless she was crazy or dreaming. She was pretty certain neither was true. While she quickly reached for the tissues to wipe running makeup from under her eye, Austin lifted up his head. He looked at her, blinking in disbelief.

"What happened?"

"You spoke to me about things only I know about," she replied, doing her best to regain her calm, professional demeanor.

Austin's eyes teared up.

"I'm so sorry. I told you they're sadists. Yours must be impatient and really wanting to taste the torment right now."

Austin gazed at her right and flinched. "You should see that asshole smiling right now!"

❧

"Could you please tell me what the fuck is going on?!" she yelled at Emmerson, after she joined him behind the one-way mirror.

"So what Klein said is true?" Emmerson was calmer than her, but also visibly shaken.

"Yes, it's true! So what's the game?! The FBI's spying on me? You rigged my house with cameras? You listen to my calls? What?!"

"Please! You know you sound crazy." Emmerson grimaced with disgust.

"What Klein just said is crazy! There's no way anyone but me would know those things! And they're all absolutely one hundred percent accurate!"

"So I guess you need to assume he's speaking the truth."

Katherine inhaled sharply in disbelief. "You're kidding!"

"Until we find out what's going on here, that is."

"Blue horses eat cotton candy," she said out of nowhere. When Emmerson bulged out his eyes on her, she encouraged him with a gesture.

"Um… chilis grow best in afternoon sun?" he said with hesitation.

❧

When Katherine returned to the interrogation room, Austin was again looking down, slanted in the chair like a ragdoll.

"Cute little exercise," he said with the same booming voice as before. "Blue horses eat cotton candy and chilis grow best in afternoon sun."

How are you doing this? she thought, now less scared and more fascinated.

"I witness you every day," Austin replied, and her heart jumped up to her throat.

You're hearing my thoughts! she said again in her mind.

"Each and every one," replied Austin. "And I put them inside his mind. Do you believe now?"

I believe, she thought. Her heart sunk with the realization that Austin Klein was not suffering from hallucinations. He was suffering from reality.

"Let him speak to me now."

The moment Katherine asked, Austin raised his head.

"Has that happened before?" she queried. "These… 'Companions' speaking through you?"

"Not that I know of." Klein shook his head. "I do not recall myself blacking out like that before. Of course, there's no way of knowing what happens to a person sleep-deprived for such a long time. You said it yourself."

"True," she spoke calmly, but was certain she was visibly shaking. And she asked suddenly, "Can you tell me about heaven?"

Klein cocked his head like a confused puppy. "I don't understand the question."

"You said that you saw what happens to people when they're dead. You said that the worse the person, the uglier the Companion, and they suffer after death according to their transgressions."

Austin's eyes began tearing up.

"Have you seen someone with a truly beautiful Companion, one that reflected how innocent and good a person was?"

"Yes," Austin's voice was breaking. "One that looked almost human, but beautiful and bright. I had such hope because of that."

"And where's that person now?"

Austin looked at Katherine with an indescribable expression. "It was Randall."

The pen Katherine was holding between her fingers fell onto the floor. Her stomach made a leap, and her heart sank into an ocean of ice.

"But you said you saw him being ripped apart!" she yelled, without any control over herself, leaning over the table. Austin didn't even flinch.

"That's just it! That's the best that can happen to you." Tears were rolling down Austin's cheeks. "Hell is much worse."

THE STAKE

I DID MANY wrongs in my life.

I know that you'd count murdering my father as one, but I wouldn't. It was a service to my mother for all the heartbreak and broken bones she suffered from his hands.

I made him suffer back. And even then, with all the hatred I had for him, I hesitated. At first. When I realized I had to go through with it if I wanted to live myself, I let all my scruples go. Can't say I enjoyed it—I treated it as a just reward for what he did to my mother and me. And I was cashing it out slowly.

Florence was a great place for me. After my father tragically died, my mother funded my university education. She never learned I was the cause of the "accident." Who would've thought one can drink enough to completely numb himself to rat bites.

During my studies I found myself more and more bored with the rubbish taught by the professors. I doubted most of the things they said, and for a good reason.

When you're not allowed to expand your mind and search freely, when your tongue must be kept on a leash so it won't slip up, when stating facts is considered treason to the established order—this is when reasonable minds doubt.

Don't get me wrong. A reasonable mind is a rare thing. Universities gather very few of them. Most people follow the rules and gobble up whatever is spewed in their direction without blinking an eye. I was not one of those.

There was one professor with views similar to mine. It took a while for him to trust me. But after he grew certain of my honest intent to learn beyond the limits of what is allowed, he began inviting me to his own house. His library contained hundreds of volumes no inquisitor would appreciate. I learned lots from the books he let me read. The main lesson I took from them: Ancient people were no smarter than contemporary ones. The amount of foolishness in these books was mind-numbing! I had a good laugh now and then, but mostly I was saddened. I thought that the look into the knowledge of centuries past would give me answers. It only gave disappointment.

But there was one volume, buried deep below a pile of discarded books. It seemed different than the others in the sense that it was handwritten. And not handwritten like those copies made in the monasteries before the invention of print. It looked like someone was taking notes of their own research. The letters were slanted, uneven, and the words sometimes bent before the edge of the sheet to not divide the word between the lines. There was no title nor author, just a leather cover and the pieces of paper between.

I asked my professor about the volume, and he was very dismissive about it. "Some foolishness," he said "I only keep it because I believe all written word has the right to exist." He allowed me to have it. And just in time, too.

Only a month later Professor Francesco Moretti was imprisoned. He'd become way too reckless in voicing his opinion that no ideas should be punishable as long as they're used to further our understanding of the world. The church proved Moretti wrong by burning him alive, alongside his book collection. Only one book survived, the one given to me.

It contained some of the notions I had encountered elsewhere, but it wasn't a mindless repeat of what others had to say. No, this author was a practitioner. And he referenced other works abundantly, pointing out mistakes and blatant myths. This was the authority I wanted to follow. The one who knew what he was talking about.

Not long after, an opportunity presented itself to try out one of his recipes. A local thief hanged for his crimes. According to the local tradition, he was hanged outside the city walls, naked, and his body left for the crows to pick clean. He was to be there for a long time. But if I was to get anything from him, I had to hurry.

The hanging was performed at dawn, so my colleagues and myself treated ourselves to the show before attending morning lectures. During the execution I was delighted to see the thief dying instantly. No suffocating to death, no comic dangling on the rope. I could almost hear his neck snap.

I attended lectures afterwards just out of a lack of other things to do. Also, my mother would be displeased with me if I shunned my education. Making my mother sad would indeed be worse than any possible punishment the university could administer for skipping lectures.

I had to wait till the very closing of the city gates. It would be much easier, I thought, to bribe the guards to let me out and come back, than to let myself be locked out from the city and try to convince them to let me in.

That evening the guards drank at my expense. I told them a story about a lover waiting for me in a country house outside the walls. The guards fully understood the need to visit a maiden in the dead of the night, when all the God-fearing men were asleep… Including the maiden's father.

The harvest that night was bountiful. Not only did I get the left hand of a thief, but there was a mandrake already blooming under his body. I paid the price for that night with my health. I had to wander outside the city walls in the cold almost until dawn, as I couldn't simply reappear after less than an hour of absence. The story I told the guards would not stand up then.

The cut hand, skillfully prepared, became my biggest helper in my future endeavors. You've certainly heard about Hand of Glory. There are many recipes, but I'm certain only mine truly works. I prepared it so each fingernail became a candlewick. Lit aflame, it rendered entire households unconscious. So many times it helped me when I needed some money. My mother was only willing to give me so much.

Mandrake has many uses, but I exceled in making fertility potions. It began with Letizia Cali, a wealthy but barren woman, wed to Giacinto Cali. Longing for male offspring that would ensure her husband's goodwill toward her, she was ready to do anything and pay any price for a way to get pregnant. In fact, two years of her marriage already passed without any success, before we had an occasion to talk during a hunting trip. I generously gave her the potion, and offered that she only pay me if she birthed a male child.

The boy she gave birth to was strong and healthy. To this day Letizia sends me valuable presents. But more important than her fondness and gratefulness toward me was her kind words about me whispered into the ears of other well-wed women. My client list grew, and soon I didn't require any more money from my mother.

But, no matter how much money I had, I always longed for more knowledge. I believe that was ultimately the cause of my doom. People can forgive greed in regards to money, but greed for wisdom disgusts them. They call you vain and insolent. They can sense their own inferiority and hence do not take kindly to those that…

AAAAAAAAAAAAAAAAAAAAhhhhhhhhhh!!!

Coherent words turned into inhuman howling as red-hot iron pricked Fabio's skin. The scream was of surprise first, pain second.

"STOP!" yelled the judge in irritation. "He was already talking, you fool!"

The torturer muttered an apology, but Fabio saw a blink of satisfaction in his eye. He decided against commenting on the obvious, that the torturer had just proven his point. He needed a moment to compose himself—this time he'd almost fainted.

"Besides my father, I never killed anyone in my life. Not directly, anyway. I had my group of faithful customers, mostly wealthy wives of nobility, also some matrons of church figures.

"They requested a poison now and then, but I always asked who the target was—if I did not agree with the choice, I'd refuse to sell it. And I admit I sometimes used my magic for my personal sense of justice. To this day I relish the memory of paralyzing and torturing a certain monk who liked the company of children a little too much. Amazing what can be inserted inside the human body, especially its rear cavities." Fabio filled the torture chamber with a hoarse laughter.

"And then I was lied to. And everything unraveled from there.

"Valentina DiMarco requested a poison. I asked her who the intended target was, as I always do. Valentina then told me about her cousin suffering greatly from the hands of her husband. The cousin was too afraid to protect herself, while the brute was becoming more violent each and every day. The abuse was so severe, Valentina said, she was scared for her cousin's life.

"Suffice to say, I was moved by that story. For years I was a silent witness to the abuse of my own mother, so I didn't hesitate and gave Valentina the poison.

"Not a week after, the dreadful news spread across Florence. The seven-month-old heir of the Federici family died in his sleep. He was found one morning, his face blue and lips black, apparently suffocated during sleep. There was no reason for a healthy baby to just die in its bed, and the symptoms described by everyone around were suspiciously similar to what my own poison would do. Furthermore, Valentina was known to be the mistress of Ludovico Federici, the child's father, which raised my suspicions even higher.

"I confronted Valentina. I'm not proud of that, but it was the first and only time in my life I struck a woman. It was only then she told me the truth. Her and Ludovico had been lovers for years, but after the birth of his heir, his lawful child, Federici's interest in Valentina decreased. Valentina could not bear her beloved's rejection and decided to dispose of its reason.

"It was obvious to Federici that the sudden death of a perfectly healthy child wasn't natural. Overnight, Valentina turned from the mistress of one of the most powerful nobles in Florence into a suspect. Torture wasn't necessary to extract the confession—desperate and teary Valentina told Ludovico the whole truth. Including the name of who made the poison."

The last sentence echoed in the torture chamber. Most members of the jury seemed bored, but not the judge. The judge had a sense of duty. He was attentive throughout the whole confession, keeping his stern expression unchanged.

"The fact that your client poisoned a different person than you thought she would does not alleviate your guilt!" he thundered. "Poison making is forbidden, and you are responsible for the deaths of fourteen people, including your father. Furthermore, we find you guilty of practicing magic, possession of books from the Index Librorum Prohibitorum, seven counts of theft, and one case of enrichment by illegal means—that is when you poisoned the prized horse of Bishop Gabbiadini so it would not win the race…"

Maniacal laughter interrupted the judge.

"You should thank me for the entertainment!" Fabio had tears in his eyes. "Not every day a horse shits itself enough to make others slip!"

Several people in the torture chamber chuckled; some of the high figures sitting next to the judge remembered that day.

The bang of the judge's fist on the table stopped the cheery mood.

"Fabio Achille Zacconi!" thundered the judge. "I sentence you to be burnt alive until your soul leaves your body! The sentence will be carried out tomorrow at dawn. And may God have mercy on your soul!"

"He never had…" murmured Fabio with a dismissive smirk.

❧

At dawn the bells tolled for Fabio Achille Zacconi. Monks from the city monastery chanted their prayers, guiding Fabio to the place of his execution. Usually people threw rotten vegetables and dead rats at those led to death, but not this time. Fabio was known for caring for those less fortunate than himself. On that day crowds of the poor and wretched gave a somber farewell to the hero.

Back in his cell, Fabio refused to give confession or pray. The good priest kept him company all the way from prison to the piazza, where the stake had been built. Riding a cart pulled by a donkey, Fabio could take a good long look at the infernal device erected in the heart of the city just for his demise. Someone took pride in stacking the pieces of wood neatly around the pole. The stake was put together so perfectly, in fact, it seemed almost sadistic, as if someone wanted to ensure Fabio would experience the best agony possible.

He didn't utter a word while he was being tied to the pole, though he shook so violently the executioner later joked that Fabio almost ripped the pole out with his spasms. When fastening him to the stake was done, Zacconi took a look at the loge built for the nobles at the far side of the piazza.

The loge was occupied by the judge and his adjutant, and also by Ludovico and Rosa Federici. These two looked like two shadows of their former selves, broken and solemn. Ludovico tried to force an expression of anger and disgust upon his face, but was too exhausted and sorrowful.

Poor souls, thought Fabio. *But let's not kid ourselves about who's the real victim here.*

The same priest who had spoken to him in prison approached him one last time to ask if Fabio needed to confess and pray, and Fabio refused once more. The priest humbly accepted his will and quickly left his side, tears rolling down his cheeks, as he knew that Fabio's soul would burn in hell, sent there, fittingly enough, with fire and smoke.

As it was customary in Florence, the judge came up to him for the last time to read his sins to his face. He recited a whole list of people who perished from his poisons, and performed a much-too-long sermon detailing what an abomination and filth Fabio Achille Zacconi was. During this eulogy, Fabio was silent and unmoving. His chin rested on his chest, his face was twitching in fear, and his heart was racing. He focused on gathering saliva in his mouth—he needed it for his last words.

"I hereby implore you to revoke Satan and beg for forgiveness!" thundered the judge. "If you do, you shall be choked till unconscious before we light the stake!" The judge looked straight at Fabio with his eyes wide open with anger and zealousness. Fabio slowly lifted his head…

And a fat, slimy blob of saliva landed straight in the judge's eye.

"Aloyshan meerarer khot!" barked out Fabio.

The judge wiped his face with disgust and looked again at Fabio, his hand twitching to strike him in the face. But he could not—the dignity of his office forbade him to do so.

Fabio smiled from ear to ear. "I was never good at haggling."

"May God have mercy on your soul!" shouted the judge before leaving the rafter upon which the stake was built. On his way to his seat, the judge nodded at the executioner carrying the lit torch.

The judge's bottom rested comfortably on velvet pillows when the stake was being lit aflame. The fire climbed quickly through the dry wood and as it started to lick the flesh, Fabio blacked out from shock. But only for a moment, as the pain woke him.

No human language can convey the sounds made by someone being burnt alive. The inhuman cacophony of pain startled the pigeons nesting at the top of the church's belltower. The smoke carried the stench.

The very moment the screams began, the judge slanted in his chair, placing his hand on his forehead, as if close to losing consciousness.

"Your Eminence?" His adjutant placed his hand on the judge's arm.

"I cannot stand the smell," said the judge, pearls of sweat running down his neck. "I need to leave..."

His adjutant aided him in reaching his office in the same piazza on which Fabio was now burning. Up the marble stairs, down the corridor adorned with tapestries, all the way to his private cabinet, the adjutant let the judge lean on him.

"Leave me be!" ordered the judge, barely reaching his armchair.

"Your Eminence, I should not leave when you're so—"

"Leave, I said!" thundered the judge in a way the adjutant knew all too well. There was no point in arguing.

The very moment the door closed after the adjutant, a violent shiver came over the judge. And then a sudden spasm threw him onto the floor.

He landed on a fluffy carpet that muffled his fall. He heard the screams through the window. The wind picked up, so death would not be so quick for the man at the stake, as the flames bent and the smoke was carried away.

"Why the pain?" he hissed through clenched teeth. His stomach churned, his muscles were like tight knots violently unraveling, and his blood seemed to boil. *What if I perish right here, right now?* he thought in panic.

But everything stopped, as abruptly as it started. The judge rose to his feet, straightened up the wrinkles on his robe and looked through the window at the piazza.

The man burning at the stake was now writhing, in vain, trying to get himself out of the bounds. He also attempted to shout, but the wind changed direction and the smoke gagged him. Well, even if he managed to say anything coherent, it wouldn't help him in the slightest.

Fabio chuckled as if it was the most delicious joke he's ever heard. Surely the judge did not expect to be pranked that day.

With contempt, Fabio looked at his new body. "New" was questionable—it was surely past its prime. And Fabio really liked his former one, but that was being burnt to a crisp. No matter! He would soon find a new, fresher one.

"Poor Judge," he murmured, seeing the man on the stake losing consciousness. "I hope he confessed today."

THE WHISPER

Aaron Blanchfield, aged fourteen, occupation: farmer. Fourth child and third son of the family of Samuel and Agatha Blanchfield. Always a sensitive child, lost in his own thoughts, and more interested in wandering neighboring forests than spending time with other people. At age seven he had learned from a local priest how to read, but lost interest in further education after he had read all the books in the preacher's library.

His natural obedience and docility made him easy to manage. He never caused trouble, did his share of work, and spent the little amount of free time that he had by himself.

Such solitary way of life was the cause of frequent teasing from his peers, but Aaron never seemed bothered by it. As he grew older, his walks in the woods became longer, and Aaron, growing accustomed to the woods themselves, ventured deeper and deeper. This tenacity was the reason for the recent tragedy.

The Whisper is a folktale originating from Aaron's home village. There is no other place in the territory of Scotland, England, Wales or the neighboring islands that has the same legend.

What the Whisper looked like, nobody knew, because those who had seen it, didn't survive the encounter. Only those who managed to avert their eyes from the Whisper returned to the village alive to tell the tale.

The Whisper targeted those who wandered the forests alone. Noises, like the rustling of leaves or a snap of a twig, were the first clue it was lurking. Some might have thought it was a wild animal at first, and they were done if they didn't close their eyes quickly enough.

Those who kept their eyes shut told how the Whisper tormented them, trying to force them to look at it. The remains of those who took a peek were found later, stuffed in the hollow of a tree or impaled on its branches like twisted Christmas ornaments. The body parts were sometimes mangled so badly they were almost mashed to a pulp, but the heads were always intact. It was as if the Whisper did the villagers a favor, ensuring they could recognize their own.

Those were the tales of the darker, more foolish times, some would say. Ways of teaching children to not step into the woods. And though most villagers claimed to not believe in the Whisper, all of them kept away from the forest. The bravest would wander around its border, picking berries, twigs, or mushrooms and leaving hastily after getting what they needed.

Aaron was the first in decades who dared (or was stupid enough) to venture deep and alone. Why his family had let him was the subject of gossip and speculation. Some believed the Blanchfields wouldn't care if their third son was dealt with by the forces of the forest. Others argued that the Blanchfields simply didn't believe in the old tales and let their son do what he wanted.

❧

"I was walking through the woods, keeping to my usual paths," said Aaron to the constable dispatched from the town to gather information about the incident. "I like to listen to what the birds have to say—they see a lot because nobody pays attention to them.

Very few people go this deep into the woods, so I find lots of raspberries and mushrooms and bring them to my mother. Sometimes it's windy and then the trees talk. I don't like that because they talk about dark things. They scare me. I have to cover my ears and scream to blot them out. But that day there was no wind and it was a lovely evening for a walk.

"I know all about the noises of the forest. I know every call of a fox, and I know the differences not only between bird species but also between individual birds. I can recognize the sound of a pinecone falling to the ground, and a hedgehog trotting through the grass. So when I heard a rustle in the bushes, I knew it was none of the usual sounds of the woods. I closed my eyes and kept walking. I hummed so the Whisper would think I didn't know it was him. I hoped he would leave me alone.

"Then I heard my mother's voice calling me for a meal. I ignored it. Then I heard voices of my brother and his friends teasing me, as they usually do, and I ignored that too.

"The Whisper tried with the voices of my father, and Rebecca, who is always so good to me. But I'm not stupid! I didn't open my eyes for a second, so I was worried that I'd lost my way. I extended my arms and with my feet I searched the ground for roots, rocks, and holes that would inform me where I was. That's how I made sure I was on the right path.

"I don't know how much time had passed before the palms of my hands touched the bark of the beech tree. There is only one growing on the way to the village, so feeling it gave me comfort. By that time the Whisper had silenced himself, but I wouldn't risk opening my eyes because his presence was obvious. I could sense a shape keeping me company, sometimes it felt like a person, sometimes like a four-legged animal, sometimes like a blur, but it was always there.

"Still touching the trunk of the beech tree with my right hand, I took a step forward. My face bumped into something. I sensed the cloth and flesh under it, like a stomach. I started to touch it with my hands—the flesh was cold and unmoving. I tried to talk to the person standing before me, but they said nothing. I reached out to their face, but before I got to it, my fingers touched the neck.

"There was a thick cord looped around it, so tight it broke the skin. Bare toes touched my thighs and I stepped back, tripped on a root and fell. I understood then why I stopped sensing the presence next to me, because it manifested right before me, giving me a reason to look at it. I didn't. I did not open my eyes, not for a moment.

"I knew I had to get out of there, but it took me a moment to compose myself. When I walked past the hanging corpse, I sensed it wasn't there anymore. I felt no presence around me, but I wouldn't dare open my eyes.

"Soon after I heard a familiar barking, Duke, our oldest dog, was always the first to greet me, venturing deep into the forest every time I was coming back home. I was so relieved; I was sure I was saved.

"I crouched before Duke and felt his moist hot breath on my face while I stroked him. He kept me company, walking by my right side while my hand remained on his back. I clenched my fingers on his thick, rough coat, to ensure I didn't lose him. We marched together in peace and silence, just like usual. I could feel the little slope under my feet, a sign we were getting close to home. My heart rejoiced and I battled the urge to open my eyes and dart toward the village.

"The moment I thought about doing that, Duke's back escaped from under my hand. He must've walked into a hole in the road. All I was left with was a clump of dog's hair. It came off so easily as if it was never attached to a body. And not only that, there was something slick smeared all over my hand. It was blood. Duke did not utter a sound.

"Terrified that he was wounded and bravely enduring the pain, I found his back again. What I touched was flesh… without skin. I dipped my fingers in blood covering exposed muscles. I ran my fingertips through rhythmically tensing and relaxing knots of meat, and the *dog* did not make a sound of protest.

"My body shuddered with a chill of horror. I was so horrified I couldn't raise my hand. So I had walked arm to arm with a monstrosity that decomposed while still moving and breathing. The terrible stench of rotting flesh hit my nostrils. I was so shocked I wouldn't take my hand away, while it sank deeper between muscles and tendons. It stopped on something hard to the touch—something that could only be bone.

"What saved me was a lone stone on which I tripped. I fell on my stomach and with disgust, wiped my hand in some dry leaves. The monster wouldn't let me be. It stopped right before me, growling and snorting, torturing me with waves of fetor emanating from its festering body. Blind and scared, I dashed through the forest, clasping my eyelids together.

"Running blind through the forest ended up in another fall. I lost my footing and rolled down the hill. It was a hazel bush that stopped me. I'm not sure how much time had passed before the dizziness went away. The pain in my ankle sobered me up.

"'I will not open my eyes, no matter what you do to me!' I yelled. 'No matter the smells, the sounds, or the touch! I will not be your victim!'

"Then a deafening whistle pierced the air. It was so close I had to cover my ears to not lose another sense. I screamed to counter the sound that turned from a whistle to a screech and then a roar. I kept my mouth open and yelled to show I wasn't afraid, but I had never been so scared in my life.

"I could sense my body sinking into the ground, cold, moist earth embracing me from all sides. The soil forced its way into my mouth, gagging me, my tongue stuck in place. I couldn't breathe, and I could not scream anymore. When the earth reached my throat, I thought it was my end.

"And suddenly I was free. Back on the surface, vomiting out the soil, frantically clearing my ears and nose.

"'Won't you stop?!' I yelled. 'I told you, I will not open my eyes! I will not let you kill me!'

"A growl answered me, annoyed but relentless. It was all around me, coming from all directions at once.

"'Enough!' I was crying at that point. I couldn't bear another torture. I just wanted to go home. But the Whisper showed me there was no way he would let me go alive.

"I felt the ground with my hands, searching among the leaves for a weapon. The thought of killing the Whisper crossed my mind, but I rejected it. How could I kill a creature that could become any form or no form at all? I had to do something else..."

The candlelight flickered in the soft evening breeze. In the room there were only four people: Samuel and Agatha Blanchfield, Aaron Blanchfield, and Constable Sullivan, who was taking notes. According to his own words later, Constable Sullivan then "took a long look at his interlocutor, saddened, feeling nothing but pity toward the lad."

"And then you found... a twig?"

"Yes. It was difficult... Nobody in their right mind would hurt themselves out of their own volition, but I saw no other way... The pain was unbearable. Possibly would have been less if I did it clean and quick, but I was hesitating. I couldn't... but... I still did..."

As proof, Aaron took off the piece of cloth covering his eyes. There were two gaping holes beneath—no eyeballs and no eyelids, all destroyed by Aaron weeks before. The scarred, red holes were a startling sight for anyone. Constable, though a man of courage, found himself flinching in disgust and fright.

"After I did this, I marched back to the village. The Whisper hasn't left me since. Perhaps he's too stupid to understand I can never see him again, or perhaps he's locked onto me since I gouged out my own eyes. I was back home after the sun set… I was feverish for the next two weeks and the doctor didn't expect me to get better. But I did. I have a new purpose now, so I have to live."

"What purpose is that, my boy?" asked Constable.

"The Whisper has not left me. He's with me day and night. I hear his taunts and whistles and growls, he nibbles at my calves, his breath tickles me in the ear. But he cannot kill me unless I see him, and I cannot…"

Mrs. Blanchfield began to sob in the corner, but her son smiled from ear to ear.

"Now people are no longer afraid to go into the forest. They even go deep enough to leave snares for rabbits and to fish in the stream. I know that some, perhaps most of them, say that the Whisper never existed, that it is an old fairy tale to scare little kids. I also know that those who speak the lowest of me—that I'm crazy and all that—go to the forest more often than anybody else. Now that the Whisper is gone, they show everybody how brave they are and how much they never believed it in the first place."

THE TOYMAKER

"DAAADYYY! I WAAANT iiit! I want it, Daaadyyy!" the whole shop had heard nothing else for the past minute, and the patrons were losing patience.

The object of desire was a ballerina doll: posable, with jointed legs and arms, pretty and perfect. The only reason nobody had bought it yet was that it was incredibly expensive.

Price was not an issue for the Marley family, and the six-year-old daughter of Mr. Marley knew it well. She had been taught that everything was hers if she wanted it.

Only today Mr. Marley hesitated. He began to explain that Lynn had too many toys as it was. So many, in fact, that she had no time to play with them, so another doll would not be…

"IIIII WAAAAANT IIIIIIIT!" another howl tore the air.

"If that girl doesn't stop, she'll drive Mr. Janacek out of town and we won't have a toyshop anymore," Mrs. Salisbury muttered under her nose.

"Spoiled little brat," murmured Jeff, one of the local teenagers, to his sister.

Unbeknownst to them, Mr. Marley heard all of their whispers—his hearing was impeccable. And he found himself angry and unable to refuse his child yet again.

He loved his daughter and wanted the best for her, but she did not need the doll. Heck, she didn't even want it! It was just another whim that would pass as soon as they got home, and the doll would be thrown into a toy chest, never to be played with.

The anger and frustration of Mr. Marley reached its peak... and left him.

"Alright," said Mr. Marley, and the whole shop became silent. Not only his daughter, but the other patrons also shut their mouths, eager to see the end of it.

"You can have it."

Little Lynn Marley triumphantly carried the ballerina doll almost as big as herself to the counter. Mr. Janacek had sat there throughout the whole commotion, not looking up even once, silent, deeply engaged in his work, sewing up a stuffed giraffe.

Mr. Janacek was in his fifties, with thick glasses, uneven teeth, and wrinkles cutting his forehead into thin slices every time he wanted to express surprise or disagreement. All in all his physique wasn't unpleasant, though it bore some signs of wear. It was his mysteriousness and distance toward others that made some people uncomfortable in his presence. But not Lynn. Lynn was too insolent to care about anybody's boundaries.

Not without difficulty, little Miss. Marley placed the doll on the counter. That was the first time Mr. Janacek looked at her.

"Thank you for bringing it to me," he said.

"You don't have to bag it," said Mr. Marley extending his hand with a bunch of bills in it.

Something was in the air. The whole toyshop went dead silent. Patrons pretended they were busy assessing the contents of the shelves, but were shooting quick glances at the three people at the far end of the shop.

"I'm sorry," said Mr. Janacek. "But it's not for sale."

The hot summer air entering the shop through an open door turned into chilling wind. Everyone's muscles stiffened. Everyone's, but not Mr. Janacek's. He seemed more occupied with his plush giraffe than with the two people standing before him.

"I'm very sorry for that… scene earlier," said Mr. Marley in his business tone. "We'll just take the doll and be on our way."

Mr. Janacek ignored him. The doll stayed where it was placed by Lynn. The toymaker didn't reach for the money, did not ring the cash register. He just kept to his work sewing up the stuffed giraffe. The chill that blew through the shop eased up a little and a few people chuckled.

"I want the doll," said Lynn. It was not a request, not even a statement. It was an order.

"You cannot have the doll," replied Mr. Janacek in a bored tone.

"Why not?!" Lynn's voice reached a high pitch.

"Because I don't like you," replied the toymaker in a perfectly calm, matter-of-fact voice.

Jeff and his sister chortled in their corner next to the plushies. Mrs. Salisbury frowned to show everyone she wasn't condoning that type of behavior, hiding her curled up lip behind the fan she carried around during summer.

Lynn stood before the counter, silent, not knowing how to react. Nobody had ever refused to give her anything. And nobody had ever told her they didn't like her. Everybody liked her. It was obvious that she was liked with her toys, dresses, and pets.

She didn't have time to figure it out, because her father took her by the hand and pulled her toward the exit.

"I'm sorry," he mumbled to Mr. Janacek and rushed outside, red in the face. Patrons' giggles bid them farewell.

❧

Mr. Janacek showed up one spring morning and settled himself in the late Phillips' house. It was a sensation, because nobody in the town knew the old place had been sold. And nobody knew Mr. Janacek.

Suddenly a carpenter's workshop became a toymaker's. Mr. Janacek lived upstairs and worked downstairs, adapted the shop to his own needs, and spruced up the place to be more inviting to customers.

Now patrons strolled among shelves carved and painted to look like castle towers, ships, and forests. They picked up plushies hanging from the ceiling in bunches like grapes. They oohed at the green fire-breathing dragon sculpted in the ceiling. They admired the pink and yellow merry-go-round softly jingling in the corner.

Mr. Janacek's toyshop was a place for everyone, not only for kids, but also for adults and even teenagers. Customers came from neighboring towns to pick up a gift for themselves or someone else, and the townsfolk soon ceased to marvel at the amount of money the toymaker seemed to have.

Despite all his wealth, Mr. Janacek dressed humbly. He also ate at Emma's, a great place to eat if you liked home cooking, but not so great if you wanted to appear fancy. Emma told other townsfolk that the toymaker always ordered the same: a piece of meat or fish, mashed potatoes, boiled vegetables, and a glass of beer.

He didn't socialize much, so even months after he moved in, everyone barely knew him. Usually the townspeople would not take kindly to recluses, especially if they came out of nowhere, but Mr. Janacek…

Mr. Janacek was different. In every possible way.

❧

He put away the giraffe plushie when Jeff approached the counter. After a long deliberation with his sister, Jeff had decided on a stuffed bear with a red bow-tie. He placed it on the counter next to the ballerina doll and reached to his pocket for money.

Mr. Janacek picked up the bear and shook his head in polite disappointment.

"Oh, this won't do at all!" he said.

"What?!" Jeff shot him a surprised glance from under his black bangs.

"It is for Christie, isn't it?" Mr. Janacek asked gently.

"Yeees." Jeff shot another glance, this time scared and ashamed.

"Well, I'm telling you this won't do at all! I mean, it's a nice gift, but Christie deserves something special, doesn't she?"

"W-well..."

Before Jeff could stutter out anything coherent, Mr. Janacek left his chair, walked up to a shelf crowded with plushies, picked one, and came back to the counter.

"She wants this."

On the counter now lay a white poodle in a blue dress with blue bows tied to its ears. Jeff picked it up and a calm sensation came over him—the dress was silky, and the white fur was so soft and fluffy he thought it could melt under his fingers. But it cost...

"I take this," said Mr. Janacek, pulling out one of the bills Jeff was clutching in his fist. The bill had a big, fat... **five** printed on it.

"But..." Jeff tried to intervene, while Mr. Janacek rang him up and hid the poodle in a brown paper bag.

"Have a nice day!" The toymaker winked at him, pushing the paper bag into his arms.

Jeff stood there, dumbfounded. He looked at Mr. Janacek, then into the bag. A smile popped on his face. He closed the bag, looked at the toymaker again, uttered, "Thank you!" and left with his sister awaiting him at the door.

ꟹ

Perry, a puny boy of ten, hid amongst the shelves, observing other people strolling around the shop. He giggled at Lynn not getting what she wanted, he saw Mr. Janacek giving Jeff the poodle plush, and was now observing Mrs. Salisbury.

She was buying another "adorable little trinket" for her "nephew in London." The trinket was a posable knight carrying a sword and a shield. She would never buy it unless she thought there was only herself and Mr. Janacek in the shop. She had an image to uphold and medieval knights were not a part of it. And obviously the knight was never to be sent to any nephew.

Perry was invisible to most people—they didn't pay attention to him, unless they wanted to tease or scold him. Most of the time he wanted to become invisible to his father, but had no such luck. He had no friends to visit Mr. Janacek's shop with, so he always came alone. He was coming only to play with one of the toys away from everybody's sight.

The crocodile toy Perry liked so much was made out of green-painted wood. Its jaw chattered, its tail wagged, and it was perfect in its simplicity. There was no way Perry could afford it, and no way for his father to buy it for him, so admiring it in the shop was the only thing he could do. Not that any other toy in Mr. Janacek's shop could become his. They were too expensive, that is, they were not free.

Playing with the crocodile in the toy shop was one of his few pastimes. He didn't like being at home, and he was teased at school and everywhere between home and school. Mr. Janacek's toy shop was the only truly safe place he knew.

He played quietly with the crocodile, making sure the wooden teeth wouldn't chatter. He was saddened by the fact that one day the crocodile would disappear from the shelf, bought by someone who could afford it.

"I'm glad you like it," a man's voice right above him made Perry jump. Mr. Janacek had approached him so quietly, the boy had no way of knowing the toymaker had moved from his spot behind the counter. Perry's first thought was to escape, but he was so terrified he couldn't move.

Mr. Janacek squatted beside him, smiling, and gently took the crocodile in his hand.

"It's one of my finest works, you know. Perfection needn't be complicated."

Perry, sitting on the floor with his legs folded, followed the crocodile with a longing gaze.

"Let's ring you up," said Mr. Janacek with a smile, standing up.

Panic came over Perry. *So this is how it ends! The toyshop—a safe haven no more! The toymaker will scold me for wasting his time and throw me out!*

With his heart jumping up to his throat, Perry followed Mr. Janacek to the counter and tried to stutter a word of protest, "M-Mr. Janacek… I… I don't…"

"Three glass pieces, please," said Mr. Janacek.

Perry blinked, stunned. He must've heard wrong.

"H-how much?" he stammered.

"**Three** glass pieces," repeated the toymaker politely.

Perry blinked again. That was exactly what he had in his right pocket, gathered at the river shore, three glass bits from shattered bottles, smoothened by the waves into tiny pebbles.

With a shaking hand, Perry reached to his pocket. He produced the requested payment—two green bits and one brown—and put it on the counter. Mr. Janacek collected them into his cash register as if they were coins.

"And this is for you!" He didn't pack the crocodile in a paper bag, but slipped it into Perry's left pant pocket. The pocket had a hole in it, so the crocodile's tail fitted right in there, and the whole toy was hidden from the sight of others.

"Thank you for your purchase," said Mr. Janacek, showing him his uneven teeth in a wide smile.

Perry walked home, still shocked from what had happened. He had the crocodile! He didn't dare reach into his pocket. He was afraid that if he tried to touch the toy, it would disappear. He felt its weight and shape his entire way home.

About twenty minutes later he arrived at the tiny apartment where he and his father resided. Perry sighed with relief realizing his father wasn't home.

He went to the kitchen and found two slices of stale bread. He also found a piece of cheese—yellow with blue spots. After cutting out the blue parts with a blunt knife, Perry made himself a sandwich, not a bad one, he had to admit.

Afterwards, Perry tried to do his homework, but resigned shortly after—he didn't understand the math, and he didn't like reading. So he took the crocodile from his pocket and played with it for the rest of the evening. It was still hard for him to believe the crocodile was finally his, but the facts could not be denied.

Father did not come home that night, which was bittersweet. Sweet, because Perry had an evening of calm and peace. Bitter, because he knew all too well what was to come.

❧

The next day was like any other. Teachers were getting angry at him for not doing his homework and not being able to answer even the simplest of questions. Other kids mocked or ignored him. He sat alone between classes and during lunch. But something was different that day; he had the crocodile now!

Beaming with joy, he rushed home after classes. But before entering the apartment building, he noticed something in the dirty, rubbish-ridden backyard.

Winona Harbor, "Stupid Winona," nine years old, was sitting in the yard. She often played there by herself, if you could call that playing. She was usually poking rocks with a stick or observing the backyard with an empty expression.

Winona didn't go to school, lucky girl! Because she was "different" and couldn't follow the lessons at all. Perry wished he could too be considered "different," and envied her a lot.

That day Winona was sitting in the backyard as she usually was, but this time she played with the ballerina doll from Mr. Janacek's shop. There was no mistaking it! A huge doll with a pink tutu and detailed makeup sat on Winona's knee. The presence of the doll in Winona's arms was by itself shocking, but there was something else.

Winona was talking to the doll. Actual coherent words were coming out of her mouth. Not mumbles, not humming, or screaming (she screamed a lot when someone tried to make her do something she didn't want to). Words!

"Hello, Winona," Perry greeted her from a distance.

"Hello, Perry!" she replied with a high-pitched voice, shaking the doll a little. So obviously it was the ballerina speaking.

"How are you today?" he asked, playing along.

"Weather nice, Mr. Bailey," Winona squeaked back.

"Does your mamma know you speak now?" Perry asked.

"Mamma knows! Mamma went for Doctor Shelley. I screamed, I didn't go," replied Winona in her normal voice.

"Yep! You would do that, alright!" Perry chuckled. He observed for a while longer how Winona played, and went back home with a smile.

The moment he passed the door his grin disappeared. Father was already home. He sat at the kitchen table, a smoked fish placed in front of him on a greasy newspaper. Suddenly Perry realized how hungry he was.

"I met your teacher today," Father said, wiping his hands on a dirty piece of cloth. "She said you didn't do your homework. Again."

Perry said nothing, because nothing he could say would save him. Whatever he did, whatever he said, it was always wrong. And the result was always the same.

"She said that at this rate you'll flunk another year," continued Father, standing up from his chair.

Perry decided to approach the issue like Winona—maybe if you don't talk to people, they just leave you alone?

A struck to the head thundered inside his skull. He blanked out for a moment and found himself lying on the floor, the room dancing before his eyes.

"No wonder your mother died! She knew what a moron you'd turn out to be and kicked the bucket to spare herself the shame!"

As Perry was unresponsive, Father left the kitchen. He went to the balcony to drink, while Perry lay on the floor for some time, the world around him spinning.

Later he crawled into his room and into his bed. Good thing the next day was Saturday. He didn't have to wake up early. He fell asleep, the world still swirling around him.

The morning wasn't the worst. Perry had a terrible migraine, but there was no blood this time. He went outside to bring a bucket of fresh water from the well—their apartment didn't have running water. He saw Winona with the ballerina doll and that image alone improved his mood. He went back to the apartment, made some tea, ate what Father had left from the smoked fish, and went to his room to play with the crocodile.

He'd barely managed to take the toy from its hiding spot, when he was startled by a scream, and a familiar one at that. Winona! This was the way she yelled in protest. Perry rushed to his window and couldn't believe his eyes: two girls were wrestling Winona to the ground, while Lynn Marley was quickly making her way out of the backyard with the ballerina doll in her hands. Without thinking, Perry dashed out of the apartment, almost rolled down the stairs as he lost his footing on the way, and stormed into the backyard.

"Leave her alone!" he yelled, bolting toward the girls who quickly left Winona and followed Lynn out to the street. A pain-filled moan stopped him from pursuing them, and terrified that Winona was hurt, he returned to her. She wasn't crying, just screaming, screaming like a mad person. She had been wronged, and she was going to inform the whole neighborhood about it! Not that anybody from the neighborhood cared.

"Are you hurt?" asked Perry. Winona stopped screaming but didn't answer him. She folded her legs so she could place her chin on her knees, and embraced them with her arms. And she froze like that, with a heartbroken expression and tears running down her cheeks.

He tried to talk to her, but she kept silent. Just like that, she'd turned back into the old, "stupid" Winona. And the only sound she made was an annoyed moan when he tried to make her stand up and go to her mother.

As Perry was out of ideas on how to help her, he went back to his apartment. And when he entered his room, he froze in terror.

Father was sitting on Perry's bed, wooden crocodile in hand. When Perry had rushed to help Winona, he forgot to hide the toy.

The stench of digested alcohol hit Perry in the face. Father was definitely hungover. And he was not pleased.

"Where did you get it?" he asked in an ominous whisper. The wooden parts clicked together while he handled the toy. Perry looked longingly at the smiling toothy face of the crocodile, its smug expression.

"I-I bought it," he replied in shuddering voice.

"WITH WHAT?!" his father roared.

The toy landed on the floor with a loud thump. The tail was the first to go under a heavy work boot. Then the head. Perry screamed and dove for the toy, but his own hand was caught under the sole of the boot. The pain was such a shock, Perry's scream got stuck in his throat. Another surge of pain, this one in his skull, sent him flying amongst the stars.

When he woke up some time later (he couldn't tell when exactly), he was still lying on the floor. He knew from the silence surrounding him Father had left for his job. Perry looked at the crocodile lying next to him and tears burned his eyes. The body of the toy was too sturdy for Father to destroy, but the tail was broken into several pieces, and the jaw was broken off the head.

Sobbing, Perry gathered what was left into a tin box and placed it under his bed.

"I'm sorry," he cried. "I should've hidden you sooner."

He wept for the rest of the day, lying in his bed. In the evening he finally fell asleep, feverish and exhausted.

He was sleeping when Daniel Bailey, his father, came back home, exhausted from working all day at the warehouse. His body was sticky from perspiration and dust, but he didn't bother washing. He took off his work boots, lay on his bed and took several sips from the bottle he was still carrying, slowly lulling himself into sleep.

At that point he was too tired and too hazy to remember what had happened that morning. He didn't remember how furious he was at his own son for stealing from others. He didn't remember how he destroyed the one *thing* giving his son joy.

But the *thing* did remember.

Deep into the night, Dan Bailey woke up. Though the window was open, the room was filled with stuffy air. This sort of a heatwave was unusual for May. But it wasn't the heat that woke him. It was a sound.

He needed a moment to understand what he was hearing in the darkness of the room. A chattering. Like the chattering of teeth, but… wooden?

Dan moved his head toward the sound and his heart skipped a beat. His bed had a metal frame and a railing at its foot. On that railing sat a toy. A wooden crocodile.

Now he vaguely remembered something about a toy Perry stole from a shop. He also remembered breaking it into splinters (not really, but he liked to think about it that way), and this thing was in mint condition. And it was looking right at him.

"What the hell?" he muttered. "He stole two of them?"

He picked up the toy and took a good look at it. It was just a bunch of differently shaped chunks of wood assembled together into an elongated reptile body. The parts of the toy clicked together when he was picking it up. It was smiling in a way most people would call funny. So why did Dan feel sweat trickling down his forehead?

Pissed at his unexplained moment of weakness, he stood up with a thought to throw this one out into the backyard. But the moment he got close to the window, the wooden thing chattered its teeth, all by itself. Dan looked down at it and froze, as the silly crocodile's expression had changed. It looked up at him in anger and whispered, "You're a terrible human being, Dan."

Startled, Daniel dropped the toy onto the floor. It slithered under the bed.

Not believing his eyes, Dan told himself that he was dreaming. Or possibly delirious from the mixture of booze and heat. He wasn't tempted to look under the bed. There was no crocodile there anyway. He was just having a terrible nightmare.

He lay back down on his bed and tried to fall asleep again. His eyelids became heavy, and he was already drifting away when the chattering woke him once more. What followed was a surge of pain.

He screamed like never before and clutched his fingers around the bloody stump of his left leg. The leg he used to crush the crocodile toy.

The blood was hosing the sheets as everything below the knee was bitten off. His calf and foot were lying next to him on the bed, oozing blood. Dan was choking on his own saliva, breathless, unable to scream, his entire body in shock. Another chatter. The toy sat on his arm. And went for his throat.

He woke up.

The sun entered shyly through the window. His pillow was moist from sweat. He heard rustling in the kitchen, meaning Perry was up. He looked at his left leg—it was there, still attached to his body. He wriggled his toes to make sure.

"It was only a dream." He sighed. His eyes burned from the sweat that dripped from his forehead. His leg was hurting. Probably because he stomped that stupid toy of Perry's. That was why he had a nightmare. Yeah! That was it!

Quite calm, he threw the sheets away to get from under them and...

There was a puddle of blood in the middle of his bed. What the hell?! With his heart pounding, he checked his left leg.

Right below the knee a fresh stitch was keeping the calf affixed to the rest of the limb. He fingered at the twine sinking and emerging from his flesh and found a mark left by a wooden tooth.

Dan bent over the edge of his bed and threw up.

~

When he entered the kitchen some moments later, he was cool and collected like never before.

His son was nibbling on an apple he had found on the top shelf. Completely surprised by his father's appearance, he froze with his teeth sunk into the flesh of the fruit.

"What happened to the... to the crocodile toy?" asked Dan.

"What... toy?" Perry asked carefully.

"The toy you bought from Mr. Janacek's toy shop."

Perry shuddered. How did Father know about the crocodile? He didn't show it to him. He hid it deep, so Father would never find it.

"What toy, Daddy?" he asked timidly, fearing the worst was coming. And he wasn't wrong. Dan didn't like to be treated like an idiot! He slammed his fist onto the kitchen table.

"Listen here, you little sh—!" A chattering of wooden teeth interrupted him. A cold shiver came over Dan's body and he turned in the direction of the noise. The crocodile toy, yesterday broken into itsy bits, was whole again and sitting on a kitchen shelf.

"How did it…?" Perry started and stopped. His father looked at the toy, then at him, then at the toy again.

"Get it and show it to me!" he ordered in a voice Perry wouldn't dare disobey. He climbed onto a chair, grabbed the toy, and showed it to his father from every possible angle, as he was told.

"So you bought it at Mr. Janacek's, didn't you?" asked Dan, and Perry nodded stiffly. "What did you pay for it?"

"Three pieces of glass."

In a trembling voice Perry explained to his father how he gathered chips of glass smoothened by the river waves and how it was enough for Mr. Janacek.

"Nice man, Mr. Janacek," commented Dan, shooting a toothy, fake smile toward the toy. "He knew you couldn't afford it, so he agreed for you to pay with whatever you had."

For the lack of a better reaction, Perry nodded once more. He was so afraid of what his father would do next.

"Well, I need to go. You're good here by yourself?" said Dan after a minute of pondering.

"Y-yes," Perry stuttered, shocked by the question and the gentle tone his father used.

"Great! See you later!" Father ruffled Perry's hair and left the flat, slamming the door on his way out.

Perry had never been so relieved. He looked at the wooden crocodile and examined it from every angle yet again.

"How did you get up there?" he asked, clearly remembering leaving the toy in a tin box under his bed. As the toy was unwilling to talk, Perry just shrugged it off.

He didn't do much of a substance that day. He mostly played with the crocodile, until he heard the familiar humming from the backyard. Winona.

Since her own toy had been taken, Perry thought she might want to play with his. He quickly left the apartment.

Winona was sitting on a wooden apple crate, her back turned

toward him. She was cradling something in her arms and humming a lullaby. When Perry walked up to her, he saw that Winona was holding the ballerina doll.

"How did you get her back?!" he exclaimed in utter shock. It was the same ballerina doll as before, no doubt about that. The same pink tutu, the painted face, jointed legs and arms.

Winona didn't respond, only continued humming her lullaby.

I guess it'll just be unexplained like how Father knew about the crocodile, Perry thought and sat down next to her. Winona noticed his wooden toy and jabbed it with her finger.

"Pet!" she said intently.

Perry smiled. "Well… it's a crocodile, so not exactly…"

"Can Pola have a pet?" she asked, jabbing her finger at the ballerina doll, then again at the crocodile toy. Without waiting for an answer, she took the doll's jointed arms, and with them, lifted the crocodile from Perry's hands. She put it on Pola's tutu, then guided the doll's arms to repeatedly stroke the wooden toy.

"Pola and pet friends!" she exclaimed, making Perry smile.

❧

On Sundays Mr. Janacek kept his toy shop closed so he could have some time to make new toys. That Sunday his work was interrupted by a thumping on the door.

"Well, I suspected I might have a guest today," he said, clearing sawdust from his clothing with a handkerchief.

Dan Bailey stood at the back door, banging on it with his fist. Most people would keep the doors closed to shield themselves from the unwanted visitor, especially a visitor so hungover, muscled, and unpredictable as Mr. Bailey. But Mr. Janacek knew the confrontation was necessary, and he preferred to have it at his own house.

"Yes?" he asked courteously after opening the door. Dan forced his way inside, pushing Mr. Janacek to the wall.

"What kind of monstrosities are you making here, Mr. Toymaker?!" asked Dan with a fake smile.

"Most people wouldn't call them monstrosities," Mr. Janacek replied calmly and politely.

"And you giving them away for free?! You're planning something, I know!"

"Mr. Bailey, you need to calm down."

"I am bloody calm!" yelled Dan. "As calm as I can be after **this** was done to me!" He rolled up the left leg of his pants to show the toymaker the stitch below his left knee.

"Don't you pretend you know nothing about it! Somehow it was your toy that did it! I will..." Dan stopped because he noticed Mr. Janacek turning his gaze away with a shy, flirtatious smile.

"Please, Mr. Bailey! I'm not that kind of man!"

A powerful blow to the head made the toymaker stumble back.

"You disgust me!" roared Dan. He noticed the basement door was open and knew what to do.

Daniel Bailey pushed the toymaker down the stairs. Mr. Janacek tumbled down and landed on a pile of cardboard boxes filled with unused scraps of fabric.

Bailey quickly descended the stairs with the intention of continuing the beating, but the moment his foot touched the basement floor, something rammed him from the side. He lost his breath and blacked out for a second. As soon as he came to, he realized a huge wooden rhino was pinning him to the wall with its horn.

He wanted to scream but was out of breath, pushed to the wall so strongly his lungs ached.

"What is this?" he squealed, barely catching enough air. "What is this thing?!"

Mr. Janacek stood up with difficulty and not without a moan of pain.

"You are a piece of work, Mr. Bailey," he said, cleaning himself from the dust from the boxes. "Apparently, we need a different approach to deal with you." He nodded at the rhino and the toy pinned Dan even harder to the wall, making it impossible for him to breathe.

"I'm afraid you won't make it to the dinner today, Mr. Bailey. Not that you planned on feeding your own son anyway," Dan heard Mr. Janacek's voice as the consciousness left him.

~

Father didn't return that morning, that afternoon, or that evening. Perry would have rejoiced but he was more than aware what came after Father's long absences.

"If you could only protect me," said Perry, drumming softly on the lid of the tin box the crocodile toy was hiding in. He fell asleep like that, with one arm hanging from the bed.

The next morning something weird woke him. A smell. He knew what it was—he'd smelled it before in the main square, from the confectionary shop and café! Cocoa!

With his heart racing in his chest, he cautiously went to the kitchen. Father was there, but somehow… different—clean-shaven, in fresh clothes, and clearly after taking a bath. He sat at the kitchen table on which sandwiches with jelly and apples cut in wedges lay on chipped, scratched plates. And there was cocoa steaming from two cheap, ceramic mugs.

"You're up," said Father in a friendly but not overly cheery voice. "Come! Breakfast is ready."

Slowly and attentively, like a homeless dog expecting to be attacked the moment it gets to a scrap of meat, Perry sat at the kitchen stool and took one of the mugs of cocoa. The chocolate sweetness made his tongue tingle, but there was no way Perry would take his eyes off his father. Strangely enough, Daniel Bailey was invested in reading the Monday issue of a local newspaper.

"I'm afraid we need to work on your grades," said Father out of the blue. "How about I help you with your homework today when you're back home?"

"H-help?!" Perry couldn't believe his ears.

"Don't stutter! I may work at a warehouse, but I finished school. I can help you."

"Yes, Father!" Perry said quickly.

"And after that we may still have some time to go to the park, would you like that?" The tone Dan Bailey used was friendly, but not overtly sweet or cheery—just a tone a father would use while speaking to his son.

In reply, Perry nodded energetically, his mouth full of bread and jelly.

"So it's settled!" Father stood and put his own mug in the sink to wash later. As he was bending over, something clicked and whirled. A weird sound, that made Perry think about a cog mechanism stuck in place. And that sound was coming from… no! That was stupid! But his father seemed to be stuck in one position.

"Father? Is everything alright?" he asked, honestly scared and worried.

A pin jumped up, a click, a whirr, and Mr. Bailey turned to his son. His face stretched in a smile that seemed forced and unnatural, and Perry could swear he heard a faint whirling sound.

"Everything's perfect, son," said his father. "Just peachy."

THE CASTLE OF BLACK

TALIA WOKE FROM her shallow sleep just in time to see the castle in its full glory. She was hanging by her wrists from a wooden frame built on a cart. The road was bumpy and sometimes branches scratched her arms, but she was so exhausted that she was falling asleep in spite of everything. What woke her was the gust of freezing wind that slapped her cheeks the moment they left the forest.

The last stretch of road was rocky and void of any plants. The castle, built entirely out of black stone, hung at the edge of a precipice. The Castle of Black.

Before that day she'd only seen it from afar—a menacing presence at the top of a mountain, glowering at the valley like a vulture eyeing an injured rabbit from a tree branch. Villagers avoided looking at it, and if they did so by accident, they quickly averted their gaze, making the sign of the cross.

Nobody knew to whom the castle belonged, how long it had been there, or how it was built so high up in the mountains. The castle was like a predator that couldn't be killed, and whose presence had to be tolerated.

If not for her current predicament, Talia would find the castle beautiful, though intimidating, with its towers piercing the clouds, gargoyles carved so masterfully you could imagine them jumping at you, arched gateways resembling a gaping mouth ready to swallow you whole.

Her sin was disobedience. A trait that others, especially men forming the village council, did not appreciate. A woman standing up to them was unheard of and had to be eradicated.

They gave her a choice: obey or be destroyed. But when a little girl was sentenced to death for being a witch, Talia could not and would not submit to the council. She knew the illness the little one was suffering from, an illness that made her shake and foam at the mouth. The little one could live with it. Instead, she was put to a cruel death and Talia was to be put to hers. The rebels had to be erased, and being left at the castle was the way for it.

No one who was ever left at the Castle of Black came back from it. People said that after someone was banished there, they could hear screams of pain carried by crisp night air. How this custom of disposing of inconvenient members of society began, nobody knew. But everyone knew the stories.

Some said the castle was a gateway to hell, and that devils resided there. Others said a sorcerer built the castle as a place to perform his black magic in peace. Either way, those left there were subjects of torture and experiments.

Talia didn't believe those tales—her mother taught her to be skeptical toward fearful stories meant to keep people in check. But Talia never expected to experience first-hand what was really happening inside.

The horse pulling her cart was the old and blind Bram, possibly the only animal that didn't panic in the vicinity of the castle. He was led by Peter, Talia's childhood friend, just two years younger than her. She suspected that Peter was asked to guide the horse because of his age—the legend of how terrifying the castle was had to be kept alive.

Several times throughout their journey up the mountain Peter tried to talk to Talia, but they were not alone. Three other men from the village accompanied them to ensure Talia would be left at the castle, not freed along the way.

Peter wasn't allowed to talk to her, but sometimes sneaked a glance at her—an apologetic, pain-filled, sometimes angry glance. He was ashamed of doing what he was being made to do, and Talia knew he was calling her stupid in his mind, and telling her off for not abiding by the council's rules. She knew exactly how their conversation would've gone if they were allowed to speak:

"You just had to oppose the council, didn't you?!"

"They wanted to kill a child. And they did kill a child. They did not have to, but people are cowards and nobody except me opposed them. So here we are!"

"You were always so stubborn! Everybody knew you'd pay for that one day and that day finally came!"

"Well, at least you won't have to worry about me from now on…"

"You truly are a fool!"

They passed the iron gates and stopped there. Peter was ordered to quickly unharness Bram. It was difficult for Talia to turn around, her wrists aching and bleeding, the skin cut by the ropes that fastened her to the frame, but as she turned, she noticed the rest of the men standing outside the gate. Their faces were contorted in anger, but it was just a facade they tried to cover their fear with.

Peter turned Bram around and on his way out he looked at Talia—a quick glimpse of farewell. This was her moment of panic.

"Wait!" she squealed before the iron plate that constituted the border between the castle and the outside world fell with an ear-piercing metallic clang.

The silence that fell after the gate somehow closed by itself was deafening. The castle was silent and still, and loneliness embraced Talia like a cold fog.

"Heeellooo?!" she yelled. "Anybody?!"

Her voice bounced from the walls of the castle, echoed between the gargoyles, and died amongst the trees in the garden.

"HEEELLOOO!!!" she yelled once more, but that sound was devoured by nothingness.

She gave herself time to listen for any sound that would betray the presence of another human being. But there was no sound. Or any movement.

She tried calling out a few more times, but no answer came. The nightfall found her still hanging by her wrists from a wooden frame on a cart. The blackness embraced her tighter and tighter until she found herself dozing off from exhaustion.

Out of nowhere, she collapsed onto the floor of the cart. She looked around in shock, but there was no one there. She glanced at the cords still dangling from her wrists—they were intact. So untied by someone? Or did they come loose by themselves?

Talia also realized something else: She could see the cords, her wrists, and everything else around her. There was light in the castle windows. All of them. The silence was still deafening, but there was light.

Talia inhaled sharply through her teeth while digging the ropes from her skin—they had cut deeply and blood had already clotted around them. After the cords fell on the cobblestones, she directed her steps toward the main entrance to the castle. The courtyard she'd been left in was only the first of three, each one bigger and richer in decoration—statues, topiaries, and flower beds.

The third, main, courtyard astonished her with fountains jetting cold fresh water. If she'd been born and raised in a higher class of society, she would've known the fountains, made entirely out of silver, were depicting Greek deities of the sea surrounded by dolphins and seahorses. The main entrance to the castle was opened wide, illuminating the courtyard with warm, welcoming light.

She entered the castle slowly and cautiously, calling out from time to time. The hall was adorned in red and gold, walls obscured with dozens of portraits, a whole army of knight's armor guarding the place. The main source of light and warmth was a fireplace so big Talia could enter it without crouching. It was what she saw inside the fireplace that made her heart drop.

The firewood was none other than the cart she was brought in. She recognized the wooden wheels and the frame she'd been hanging from just a few minutes earlier. How could this be?

Hoping the answers would come later, Talia focused on following the path marked by a red carpet. It guided her between displays of armor and weapons up to the dining chamber. Inside was another enormous fireplace with flames roaring, and a long table almost bending under the weight of all the dishes displayed on it. At the table there was only one chair, so rich and complicated in its design it could have served as someone's throne.

Talia walked slowly along the table and admired the dishes that made her mouth water. There were all kinds of meats, from domestic poultry to venison and wild boar; different kinds of fish and strange deformed creatures hidden inside hard shells; soups, fruits, and cakes she couldn't even name. When she walked up to the chair, it moved away from the table by itself, as if someone was pulling it to help her sit down.

She froze in place. For the lack of a better reaction, she said, "Hello?" again, and looked around, but there was nobody.

Cautiously she sat in the chair and frantically looked around again, when it pushed itself back toward the table.

The smells of all the delicacies piled in front of her didn't allow her to concentrate on weird happenings. She was so famished! She wouldn't forget though that she was in the castle from which nobody came out alive.

She would not touch the soup or wine, because she imagined their flavor could easily obscure the taste of poison. She decided upon an apple, on which she nibbled carefully, chewing for a prolonged time to assess the taste. Roasted duck looked so tempting! And it smelled so good! But it was drowning in cranberry sauce, so Talia deemed it unsafe. She chose a chicken leg that had almost no seasoning except for salt and pepper. Water was her drink of choice.

The dinner, however humble, took quite a long time. Talia was taking small bites, mashing them between her teeth for minutes before swallowing. It was torture, but a necessary one.

"Good evening!"

The first human sound she'd heard in the castle was so sudden, Talia jumped up in the chair before turning to the person standing beside her.

The figure and the voice were definitely female, and the person was dressed in servant's clothing so luxurious the people in the village would mistake it for queen's attire. But the submissive and humble attitude of the person disclosed her as no queen. The hair of the woman standing before Talia was hidden under a little round cap, and her face…

Was hidden under a mask. A white porcelain mask with holes for the mouth and eyes.

"Good evening," Talia replied.

"Did Milady enjoy her dinner?" asked the servant, making a little curtsey.

"Yes, quite," said Talia after the few seconds she needed to realize that the servant was addressing **her**.

"Milady, follow me to your resting chamber."

So Talia followed. In spite of all the anxiety and wariness, she was very sleepy. It didn't feel drug-induced, however, but like the very natural tiredness caused by her recent experiences.

"I'm sorry. I didn't catch your name," she addressed the servant.

The woman didn't respond and they treaded forward in an awkward silence.

"What should I call you?" Talia repeated.

The servant turned her head slightly in her direction. Her

voice was weak and carried a note of fearful warning. “Milady should not call me at all.”

The chamber that was to be Talia’s bedroom was spacious with high and wide windows exposing the entire room to the blackness outside. The fireplace was of usual proportions and the fire was weak and slowly dying. The ceiling was so high, it was drowning in darkness, and the bed was big enough for two or even three people and had canopy poles but no canopy. That was what Talia managed to notice before the servant asked her to raise her arms.

“What for?” asked Talia.

The servant turned her gaze toward a white and pink spot on a heavy, crimson quilt. Upon closer inspection, Talia realized that the white and pink spot was a nightgown.

“I wish to aid Milady in changing her clothes,” said the servant with a little curtsey.

Talia looked at her like at a crazy person. Of course she’d heard about nobility having special clothes for sleeping. She was used to working and sleeping in the same clothes, unless she decided to sleep naked. But that was not the reason she decided to oppose. She was a prisoner, she had no doubt about it, so the way she was being treated was suspicious to her.

“I don’t think so. The clothes I have are sufficient for sleeping.”

The servant hesitated for a while, apparently surprised by Talia’s reply. Finally she curtseyed, wished Talia a good night, and turned to leave the room.

“Wait! When will I meet the master of the castle?”

“Master of the castle, Milady?” repeated the servant in a polite voice.

“Yes, someone to whom this castle belongs.”

The porcelain mask made reading the servant’s face impossible, so Talia couldn’t interpret the woman’s moment of hesitation.

“The castle belongs to itself, Milady.”

That statement baffled Talia so much she said nothing more and allowed the servant to leave.

She used the last ounces of energy she had left to explore the room. The very first thing she checked was the window, but the only thing she saw through it was absolute blackness. The fire was slowly dying, and there wasn't any spare wood to feed it, so Talia couldn't explore too much. She reasoned that if she hadn't been killed yet, it was unlikely that she would be murdered in her sleep. So there was always morning.

With difficulty, she burrowed herself under a thick quilt. She didn't like it—it was so heavy it virtually trapped her like a boulder fallen upon a rabbit.

❧

When she woke, the room was drenched in darkness. The fire had died out completely, and only a dim cold starlight entered the room through the window. The furniture became indistinct shadows and Talia, not knowing the layout of the room yet, focused her gaze on a blur standing in the corner, her muscles tensing and heart racing, only to realize that she was looking at an empty birdcage.

She lay on her right side, facing the window, her back turned to the door—goosebumps crawled up her spine when she realized that. But before she changed her position, the door creaked. It was almost inaudible, but when one's senses are heightened from fear, a small squeak sounds like a roar of a bear. And then there were steps.

First distinct, on a wooden floor, then muffled by the carpet, slow, deliberate, like an escalating threat. Coming… closer…

Talia's skin was tingling, her muscles locked in place. She was paralyzed while it… stood… behind… her back.

She tried to jump out of bed, launch herself away from the figure that towered over her. She could not. Each of her limbs froze in place, her stomach tied in a knot. While danger lingered, she turned into a block of ice, cold, unmoving, but not as invulnerable.

Go away! Go away! GO AWAY! she repeated in her mind, clenching her teeth, pressing her eyelids so tight her head ached.

A set of cold fingers caressed her cheek…

She woke up with a yell of dread, bolting from under the quilt. Her leg got tangled in the sheet and Talia fell on the floor chin first, bruising her right knee and hurting her wrist as she tried to break the fall with her hand.

She was alone in the room.

She freed herself from the sheets and quilt and sat on the carpet, tears rolling down her cheeks. It was a gray fall morning, overwhelming human souls with its gloom. But still a morning, still brighter than the night. The figure behind her back… was it just a dream?

Talia touched her left cheek, the one the intruder had caressed, and her heart skipped a bit when she noticed something smeared over her skin. She looked at her fingers. They were black. She sniffed her fingertips—blood mixed with mud. She shuddered, fully and consciously realizing that the intruder in her bedroom was real.

The door creaked, and the masked servant entered the chamber with a curtsey.

"Good morning, Milady. I hope your sleep was restful."

"Not exactly," replied Talia, eyeing the servant. "I'm curious if you know anything about it."

"About what, Milady?"

"About someone coming to my room and marking my face with this!" Furious, Talia showed the servant the dirt on her fingers.

The servant seemed unfazed by Talia's outburst. She blinked quickly under her porcelain mask and turned her gaze away. She then spoke in a tone that Talia was all too familiar with, "I shall bring Milady warm water to wash."

Under a thin layer of gentleness and indifference hid a plea. The plea of a vulnerable creature not wanting to get hurt again. Talia realized how terrified the servant really was.

❧

At breakfast Talia once again ate carefully and slowly, judging the taste of every bite, every sip, feeding only on the simplest of food and drink. The servant tended to her, proposing many exotic dishes Talia had never heard of. She refused all of them—they smelled heavily spiced, making the potential poison undistinguishable in the taste. The moment the servant was distracted, Talia snatched a knife and hid it in the strip of fabric she used as belt.

After the meal she was left to roam freely around the castle. How many people before her had marveled at the riches displayed there? How many of them survived the first night? These were the questions she asked, looking for possible ways of escape. She wandered around nonchalantly to not give away her true intentions, but she felt watched.

There were two types of window in the castle: those that opened to courtyards and inner gardens, and those that opened to the outside. Talia thought about finding a rope or tying sheets together to lower herself from a window down to freedom. This plan was quickly discarded when she found out that all the windows opening to the outside opened to a precipice so deep she could not see its bottom.

She also returned to the iron gate—she wanted to be sure she checked each and every possible route of escape, even the unlikely. The iron gate was a solid plate of metal without even a lid to peek on visitors. It was like the castle was built to completely isolate the inside. No way out and no way to see outside, the building was so high up there was nothing to look at except for cloudy skies above and below.

Her walks around the castle took her an entire day and in the evening she found herself once again at the dinner table. And after the finished meal, back in her chamber, the servant presented her with a ball gown. It was a marvel in gold and navy, adorned with stones Talia couldn't even name, made out of fabric that was soft and slick. She was enchanted by it.

Until the last conscious part of her mind woke Talia from her daze.

"What is it, exactly?" She turned to the servant.

"Your ball gown, Milady."

"A ball for who? I haven't seen anybody around!"

"There are other people in this castle, Milady, I assure you."

"Truly?" Talia scoffed. "And where is this ball being held?!"

"Why, in the ballroom, of course." The servant seemed slightly amused.

"Where?!" Talia repeated in a tone that meant she needed instructions, not ridicule.

"Milady should follow the music."

Angry, Talia stormed out of her room. Indeed she could hear the music the moment she opened the door, and she rushed down the corridor.

"Wait!" the servant yelled after her in panic. "Milady should not go there without her ball gown! It's not safe!"

Talia ignored her completely. Like a beacon set up for her, the music guided her two floors down, right to white closed doors. Panting and unexplainably angry, she pushed the door. And froze.

The ballroom was crowded with people dancing to the music whose source she could not see. Gowns and coats, silks and velvets fluttered through the air like butterfly's wings, jewelry made out of diamonds, sapphires, rubies, and emeralds twinkled in the light of chandeliers. Every person dancing before her had a porcelain mask affixed to a handle of ivory and silver. They held the handles delicately between their fingers dressed in silk gloves, twirling them to the rhythm of the music, swirling them around as a part of the dance, or putting them up to their faces. At least that's what they were supposed to do, judging from their movements. Because they had no faces, or heads, only bloody stumps of necks.

The shock choked the scream in Talia's throat. She did not utter a sound and yet…

The music ceased on a false note and everybody, like a swarm controlled by a higher power, turned to her. These porcelain masks… weren't like the one her servant wore. These ones moved! They mimicked human expressions and the expression displayed on them then was of surprise and annoyance.

A thousand voices drummed in the chamber, "Why aren't you wearing your ball gown?"

She made a step back and the door behind her slammed. She fingered for the doorknob, not turning her gaze from the crowd of headless, masked monstrosities slowly approaching her. She jerked the doorknob several times without success, while they made a few more steps, the expression of surprise turning into an expression full of anger.

"Why aren't you wearing your ball gown?" they repeated, their voices higher pitched, hissing like snakes.

"Just let me go! Please!" Talia did her best to sound brave, but her voice broke.

A roar bounced off the chamber walls, filling the room with a drumming, deafening echo. All the porcelain masks twirled to display an expression of pure fury. Talia barely managed to pull out the knife she had hidden in the fabric of her belt. She was pushed, pulled by her hair, someone tore off a piece of her dress, someone else scratched her cheek. And Talia swung her knife left and right.

She succeeded in cutting several attackers—she saw no blood, but she heard screams of pain and surprise. And then she was pinned to the wall and raised high, by a ghoul who caught her by the throat in attempt to choke her. Panicked and furious at the same time, Talia targeted the bloody stump of his neck.

She stabbed three times before the ghoul let her go. And just as they'd attacked her together, now they backed away together, with wheezes, screeches, and hisses. They merged with the shadows and sank into the walls. And just like that, she was alone again.

With difficulty, she returned to her bedroom. The servant helped with cleaning the wound on her cheek, she brushed her hair and announced that a small lock was lost but with the hair combed in a proper way it was not visible. The servant offered to sew up her dress, but Talia decided to do it herself.

An hour later, still shaken, Talia drifted off to an uneasy sleep, her knife back in the folds of her clothing.

She was woken by a sound. With the first glimpses of consciousness, she caught the sound of the door creaking open. This time, though, she had the knife.

The steps again. On the wooden floor. On the carpet. A breathing. Right… above her.

But this time she was ready. Her knife was in her hand, fingers wrapped tightly around the handle. This time she would not be terrorized.

As the breathing above lowered itself to her ear…

Her muscles sprung like a trap, her arm made a small arc in the air, aimed at the face of whoever was tormenting her. And the blade…

The blade hit the pillow.

She jumped out of the bed, knife still in hand, looking for the trespasser. There was nobody except her and the last few smoldering pieces of wood in the fireplace giving her the last of the dimming light.

She was on edge. She must've imagined she heard someone entering the chamber. The door wasn't even open. She must've dreamt it. Maybe reality and figments of imagination mixed together to give her a hallucination of an exhausted brain. She went back to bed.

Talia turned the pillow cut side down so not to cover herself in feathers. She put the knife back where it belonged, and turned once again on her right side. While slowly drifting back to sleep, she thought that she should start sleeping on her left side to face the door. Or switch the position of the pillow to the foot of the bed, so she could sleep comfortably and still diligently. Her eyes itched from incoming sleep, gaze idly slipping from one corner of the room to another. Up to the window. Someone was sitting there, on the windowsill.

With a scream, she woke on another gray and gloomy morning. She was, again, alone in the chamber, this time for real. No pale face stretched in a smile. No eyes sunken in a dark, deep eye sockets. There was something else, though. A smudge of blood and mud mixed together on the windowsill.

❧

At breakfast she was tired as never before. Was there no rest in this castle? She was not safe, no matter the time of day or night.

As usual, she ate and drunk carefully. No matter the dishes the servant presented, Talia took only the simplest of foods.

"Milady may eat and drink whatever she likes," the servant commented. "Nothing here is poisoned. It doesn't need to be."

Talia could hear the smile the servant said that with. Something broke inside her. The chair fell backward and Talia launched herself at the servant. Her fingers wrapped themselves around the edges of the porcelain mask and jerked. But only a little. Not that Talia didn't have the strength to tear the mask off, but it was... attached to the flesh. By what means, she did not know. But it was like attempting to open a lid on a heavy iron chest. Not expecting the weight that worked against her muscles, Talia let go.

The servant was now screaming in pain, pressing the mask to her face. Blood trickled from under it in two thin streams.

"I'm sorry!" Talia snatched a clean napkin from the table and placed it on the servant's chin to clean the blood. "I am so sorry! It's this place! I just don't know what's next! I just… I just want to go!"

"I'm sorry as well, Milady," said the servant. "I'm… not myself sometimes."

They both looked at each other, kneeling on the floor by the table.

"I… I understand your longing to leave this place, Milady. All of us do, including those who attacked you yesterday."

"So what do I do? How do I convince the castle to let me go?" asked Talia with tears in her eyes.

"Milady cannot."

"So how do I escape?"

"Milady cannot."

"So what is there to do?!" Talia squealed.

"Accepting your situation is the only thing I can advise."

"Accept!" Talia scoffed with terror in her voice.

"Happiness is subjective, Milady," said the servant in a fearful voice. "Happiness can be whatever Milady decides."

That evening Talia went to bed with dread in her heart. She asked if the servant could stay with her and the servant shook her head. Talia asked then if she could add wood to the fire so it could last longer, and the servant said no to that as well.

So it began. Another night of uneasy sleep, filled with footsteps and breathing. Were they imaginary or were they real? She couldn't tell. She only knew she was being awoken time and time again, swinging her knife frantically around, and when she tried to go back to sleep, the smallest sound would jerk her fully awake. She looked around the room and tried to distinguish if there was someone there with her. The door, the window, the fireplace, the armchair. Where else could another monstrosity emerge?

During one such frantic survey, she turned on her right side again to check the window and the fireplace. And she heard the door creaking open. Not for the first time that night. And the footsteps again—on the floor, on the carpet. And breathing. Again. Different than the ones before, softer, less obvious. That must have been it! That must have been an actual threat!

As the breathing neared her bed, and when the hands began to press the sheets surrounding her, she struck! The blade sank in the flesh and grated the bone. A perfect strike between the collarbone and the neck. But when Talia looked in the eyes of the person she'd hit…

The moon emerged from between the clouds to illuminate the scene she'd caused. The servant's eyes dimmed behind her porcelain mask. She didn't utter a sound, though she tried. A single tear shone in the corner of her eye. And she sunk on her knees, slipping from the kiss of the blade.

Talia looked upon the effects of her attack with an empty expression. She'd have been mortified just a few days ago, but now she couldn't find any care in her heart.

She didn't check for the pulse, because there was none to begin with. The servant did not stand up—apparently losing life for the second time was enough to lose it for good. There was nothing Talia could do.

She hid her blade in between the folds of her dress. She took the dead body beside her bed by its legs and dragged it to the window. She opened it, and with huge difficulty (she was never particularly strong), she dumped the body outside. She heard it bumping on the protruding rocks, but didn't hear it reaching the ground, because the ground was so far away.

Talia closed the window and went back to bed. Covering herself with the heavy quilt, she hoped the attractions would end for the night; she really needed some sleep. She was so fed up with all the nonsense.

~

Many yards below the castle's window a woman in a porcelain mask lay on the rocks, her white visage cracked, limbs crooked, and blood leaving her body and mixing with mud. The woman wheezed with effort, unable to move. After the initial shock, her body began experiencing the pain of the fall. Her trembling fingers caressed the sharp blades of dry grass and the hard and cold surface of the rock she lay on. Icy winds flogged her body. She felt every pebble under her abdomen, and her view was gray clouds and the ground right under her nose. She couldn't die—she'd tried so many times before. And now she couldn't move, either. And yet, she was free. She was no longer inside the castle. She was out of its power.

"Happiness is subjective, Milady," the woman whispered to herself, a single warm tear leaving her eye. "Happiness is whatever I decide."

THANK YOU

Thank you for reading *Bleak*. If you enjoyed it, recommend it to another horror fan or leave a comment on Amazon or Goodreads.

ABOUT THE AUTHOR

J. Parker got the idea for *Bleak* at an art gallery. The stillness of painted figures and their inability to change their fate seemed to her bleak indeed. An avid horror fan since her teens, she decided to turn that impression into her debut collection of stories.

www.ingramcontent.com/pod-product-compliance
Lightning Source LLC
LaVergne TN
LVHW041107150826
845673LV00007B/1953

* 9 7 8 8 3 9 6 4 6 8 9 1 8 *